# The Ride From Kingston To Montego Bay

Deborah Mboya

authorHOUSE®

*AuthorHouse*™
*1663 Liberty Drive*
*Bloomington, IN 47403*
*www.authorhouse.com*
*Phone: 1-800-839-8640*

*Published by AuthorHouse 1/21/2013*

*ISBN: 978-1-4772-8007-2 (e)*
*ISBN: 978-1-4772-8008-9 (sc)*

Special thanks to the Vermont Studio Center in Johnson, Vermont for awarding me the writers residence and fellowship in October 2009 to study for the completion of this book.

# CHAPTER 1

Call me Aghagbolu, "out of war peace comes." I am the great-great-great grandson of Obi Okonya I, an African king who was crowned by Obis who had the collective right to choose the next candidate to become a king before presenting him to the village of Mbubu in Iboland. The village was ruled by over eighteen Obis who lived along the banks of the Niger River more than 150 years ago. It was powerful in war and in magic, and its priests and medicine men were feared in all the surrounding country. Obi Okonya I was a war-like man who was well-known throughout his village for going to battle against neighboring people and one of the most fearless warriors of his time. Obi Okonya II was crowned the king when he captured a leopard. Obi Okonya III was crowned the king when he proved that he was skillful at answering questions about the customs and traditions of kingship. My grandfather, Obi Ezeukwu, was crowned the king when he proved that he was skillful at answering questions about kingship. My father, Obi Mberekpe, inherited the throne because of the achievements of his ancestors. The first European traders who reached the village of Mbubu discovered African trading vessels from the African coast conducting business with Obi Okonya I for negro slaves. From that day forward, trade companies and merchants would gather together and talk for long periods of time about building and operating factories and huts that could be changed into forts – buildings to be used as a means for trade activities. Obi Okonya II organized the African Company to sell hundreds of his negro slaves to different countries all over the world. Trade companies from all over the world reached the Niger River on vessels with contracts for Obi Okonya III to sign for the sale of negro slaves to work on the Carribean sugar plantations. Obi Ezeukwu ordered his negro slaves to build him factories and forts. Obi Mberekpe ordered his negro slaves to build him a castle.

Men who wanted to become members of the upper-class, rich politicians, earned the highest title, a king. A king opened up each day in the village like an usher in a church. He decided on the number of days in a week, the number of weeks in a month, and the number of months in a calendar year. He participated in all ceremonies and festivals throughout the year, and his presence at those gatherings determined the seasons of the year. He was the ruler of a royal house that was rich enough to collect wealth, people, and power throughout the community and trading companies from other nations, but there were conflicts, different ideas, between kings and kings, kings and chiefs, and royalty and the community. In order to prevent rebellions and wars, there was always an ingathering of the government and the people to give them an opportunity to express their opinions about the Obi.

"Who has the right to choose a king?"

"There is no definite rule for choosing the next Obi."

"One king always follows after another king."

"The simple man of yesterday can become a king today."

"He must also possess the mystical power of kingship."

"The choosing of one king after another king should be done by contests."

"A contest will give a king an opportunity to compete with a candidate for the throne."

"More than one king from one royal house gives them an advantage over other kings."

"The making of a king is a national concern."

"There can be as many as three or more candidates, people who want to be a member of an office, for an Obi."

"There can be as many as three or more candidates who can be chosen to become the next Obi."

"Each royal dynasty should supply a candidate for an Obi."

"The candidate for a king must pay back any money he has borrowed."

"The candidate for a king should be wealthy."

"The candidate for a king should prove that he can earn a title as a member of one of the title societies."

"The village of Mbubu is not even big enough to consider having more than one king."

"It is customary to have more than one king."

"There should be a number of qualified candidates to choose from."

"The missionaries are against too many kings."

"That is because they want a king who is a follower of the missionaries."

"The missionaries, traders, merchants, and churchmen argue that it is impossible to serve many masters."

"We should not have to meet with missionaries to discuss the kingship of our own village."

"Meetings with these people to discuss the Obi are ignored by townspeople."

"The people should have an opportunity to consider the best person before putting them up for selection."

"The Obi is supposed to select his son to continue the program of kingship."

"The Obi is free to will his throne to any of his sons by pronouncing it so."

"A male relative should take charge of the affairs of the palace and hold the throne."

"It would make the king look more powerful to appoint powerful people to the throne."

"One candidate should be selected from one of the three royal houses in the community."

"The throne can never be left vacant."

"There should be no elections."

"The rulers do not become kings in the same way."

"The successful candidate to be crowned the next Obi is the one that wins the support of the majority of the people."

"People want to use force as a way to settle conflicts."

"To take measures into your own hands is not the answer to choosing the next king."

"We must be careful how we choose between candidates for the title of king to avoid a war."

"There are very powerful war chiefs who are willing to rush into a war if their candidate is not chosen."

"A man who is rich enough can buy a title and slaves to build up an army."

"A man's army has to be strong and powerful enough to do what he wants to do in the state and outside of it."

"There are four states on the east of the Niger River that govern the choice of a candidate the same way."

"A candidate for Obi must be able to identify the generations of his family."

"A candidate for Obi has to be able to answer questions about the customs and traditions of kingship."

"A candidate for Obi has to be able to answer questions about kingship."

The Obi's council would sit as frequently as four to seven

days of every week at a cabinet meeting and discuss their customs, traditions, and kingship in the spirit of healthy competition. Each dynastic group tried to outdo the other group in good government, healthy administration, and popular policies. All of the rulers spoke very confidently at the Obi council meeting during the discussion about how they felt towards one another.

"Meetings are being rescheduled at will to suit the arrangements of the Obi without asking other Obis."

"The Obis are calling on us when they desire to have a meeting."

"They do what they like to do in all matters."

"Some of the Obis move around against our customs."

"There are people in the community who represent the Obis better than others."

"We have Obis in this meeting who are here because they feel attached to the Obi who has brought them here."

"Some of us are respected by the community for our education."

"Other Obis are not as effective as Obis who had mother's on their side of the family to be a king."

"Many of us have made it this far because of who we know."

"Most of us have made it this far because of how much money our families have."

"There are Obis who are approached more fearlessly than others."

"In the non-dynasty kingdoms, the villages produce three out of six Obis."

"In the dynastic kingdoms, the villages produce two out of three Obis."

"Competition still remains in the different dynastic groups."

"Some Obis are more responsible than others in matters concerning the removal of Obis from an office."

"Some Obis make better decisions than others."

"There are Obis who believe that the government will support them."

"They feel self-confident while others lack confidence."

"How do you feel about taking a title away from an Obi?"

"A title should be taken away from a man who is not worthy of the title."

"How do you feel about dismissing an Obi from an office?"

"I would dismiss an Obi from an office if working with him is too difficult."

"How do you feel about taking a title away from an Obi for stubborness?"

"I would consider such action to be unfair."

"How do you feel about associating with people who have no royal blood in them?"

"He is an Okpalabisi-made Obi."

"What is the benefit of a test of your knowledge of the laws of the land?"

"To find out if we are as knowledgeable of the trained laws as we are the customary laws."

"How do you feel about the older men keeping their titles?"

"It is a tradition to replace an older Obi because of his age."

"How do you feel about the responsibility of buying a title?"

"Money can be taken away from you, heredity cannot."

"How do you feel about Obis being recruited on the basis of favor or power to make an appointment?"

"He is a "person from the sky." People are afraid of him."

"How do you feel about the Obis who attend these meetings?"

"They are very interested in the qualifications for the highest seat of power in the community."

When Prince Okonya II wanted to become an Obi in the village of Mbubu, a titled man was a person who could capture a leopard and return with his head or the leopard's jawbone. Before he captured a leopard, he had to be freed from any danger by which having to capture a leopard would be placed upon him. He was escorted to the Royal Palace by the members of the title society where he had to spend a period of twenty-four days in order to be purified from the shedding of the leopard's blood. As a candidate for the throne, he had to say "farewell" to non-royal duties such as sweeping the compound with a broom, going into the rainforest to climb a palm tree with a rope around his waist for palm-oil, and chopping firewood with an axe before he called on the members of the royal family to make the arrangements for a cleansing ceremony, his installation, his crowning, and he had to attend a meeting with the members of the title society.

"I am interested in becoming the next Obi," Prince Okonya II said.

"Because your father is the present Obi, you are privileged to become the next person to become a king."

"Now that you have informed us about your plans, the installation ceremonies can take place."

"Your enthronement has to be done in three stages."

"You have fulfilled the obligation of the first stage of becoming the next Obi."

"Now you must state your willingness to do the job well."

"Then you must perform certain rituals at one of the shrines, a place of worship."

"After that, you can become an Obi."

"That has always been the tradition of the ancestors."

The sacredness, holiness of kingship, was always expressed in rituals. As a candidate for the title of king, Prince Okonya II had to go to the ancestral shrine of past Obis where he was taught the duties of kingship before a priest. He had to cross the Niger River in a war canoe to get to the Mkpitime Lake for the ritual to protect him from the shedding of the leopard's blood. He carried with him a sword that he used to capture the leopard, a canoe paddle with a palm leaf wrapped around it as a symbol of protection, an eagle's feather as a symbol of achievement, a leopard jaw bone which was tied to the paddle, and a red band across his shoulder with a bell attached to it – red being a symbol of bravery. He offered sacrifices of food to the gods at each one of the shrines, and the members of the Royal Palace carried kola nuts, tobacco, yams, palm-oil, and white clay to offer as a sacrifice to the gods at the shrine.

"Chi, I promise to uphold the traditions of the land."

"Chi, I promise to rule the people to the pleasure and spirits of the ancestors."

"Chi, I promise to rule the people to the best of my ability."

"Chi, I promise to return to the Mkpitime Lake every three years to worship you."

"Chi, we pray for the success of the ceremony."

"Chi, we pray for the guidance of the ancestors."

"Chi, we pray for the protection of the Obi elect."

Prince Okonya II was carried from the ancestral shrine

back to the Royal Palace by his subjects as the crowd of followers cheered him on as the "all powerful king."

"Obulu Eze Ayo!" "He is the king, oh yes!"
"Obulu Eze Ayo!" "He is the king, oh yes!"

After the cheering from the crowd was finished, Prince Okonya II stood before the prime minister of the kingdom to answer questions.

"Will you use your office of king to govern well when you are crowned the king?"

"Yes."

"Will you respect the traditions of the people?"

"Yes."

"Will you terrorize, frighten, the poor?"

"No."

"Will you work towards the good of the people?"

"Yes."

"Do you promise not to break the rules of society?"

"Yes."

"Do you promise to pay back any money you have borrowed before you are an Obi?"

"Yes."

Then the prime minister held the ofo, the emblem of political and ancestral authority, in his hand and struck it on the ground before he said, "Now state the punishment for breaking any of the rules of office."

"The ofo will prosecute me."

"This ofo," the prime minister said as he presented it to him, "belonged to the last king."

"You are to keep it, and pass it on to the next king."

"Let the ofo symbolize the power and authority that goes with Obiship," said one of the king's royal servants as they beat the royal ufie drums.

The last ceremony that took place was for Prince Okonya II to answer to a court of Obis who asked him four times, "Where is the leopard?" "Where is the leopard?" "Where is the leopard?" "Where is the leopard?" Obi Okonya I, who was sitting on the throne, took out his sword and Prince Okonya II took out his sword. After striking their swords four times, Prince Okonya II had to kneel down before Obi Okonya I so that he could put a large cloth over his shoulders and place the crown, a red cap, on his head with his eagle's feather attached to it. The leopard that he captured was carried into the kitchen of the Royal Palace where it was cooked and served as the main dish at a banquet to honor the new Obi. After the throne was covered with the leopard skin, Obi Okonya I said to Prince Okonya II, "You are made a king today by me." There were still conflicts in the village of Mbubu about the crowning of a king.

"Who has the right to crown a king?"

"There is no definite rule for crowning the next Obi."

"An individual must have the right to crown the Obi."

"There are certain rituals involved in the crowning of a king."

"More than one Obi can be crowned at the same ceremony."

"Three candidates can be crowned at the same time."

"Once an Obi is on the throne, he should remain in office for a period of three years."

"After three years, the office should be passed on to the next person according to his age."

"The second eldest Obi takes his place."

"We can crown three or four Obis at once."

"As many as thirty-nine Obis can claim the right to the throne when three or four Obis are crowned at one time."

"We are talking about something that can last forty years or more."

"It is impossible to determine the number of years one Obi has been crowned before another one."

"The elders say that every Obi who wore a crown was crowned for a period of fifteen years or more."

"The village of Mbubu crowned more than eighteen Obis before Obi Oknoya I."

"Those Obis were members of the four royal clans of the king."

"Of the four royal clans, only one has tried to control the crowning of an Obi."

"The first Obi was a member of a clan that produced more Obis than any other royal clan."

"That should be enough to determine who crowns the next Obi."

"Nobody except an Obi has the right to be crowning another Obi."

"Crowning can be done by kings who perform ritual ceremonies at the shrine."

"The crown should be offered as a sacrifice to the ancestral shrine."

"Obis of the past wore the red cap as a symbol of their connection with royalty."

"A king must consult with a diviner to make sure that his crowning is accepted by the spirits of the ancestors."

"There are kings who left the shrine, came out, were placed on the throne, and crowned the next Obi."

"An Obi has to crown another Obi."

"No one else has a right to crown another Obi."

"The next of kin cannot crown an Obi."

"That would violate the rules of succession to the kingship."

"The prime minister of the kingdom is the next highest official to the Obi."

"He is the one who communicates decisions to the Obi."

"He has the right to appoint and install chiefs in the absence of the Obi and crown the new Obi."

"The traditional ceremonies have to be performed by the candidates before they have the right to crown an Obi."

"The candidate must also make sure that his kingship brings wealth to the whole community."

"Some of the Obis in the past proved to the community that they were not responsible enough to become a king."

"We must crown the candidate who makes his actions known to the state council members and the people."

"When an Obi is not responsible for the office, the people have the right to give his office to another clan."

"There are so many conflicts to deal with crowning a king."

"A person can take action in a native court against an Obi if the people question who can wear the crown."

"Some people challenge the right of the Obi to use the crown."

"People spread rumors throughout the village about who has the right to the throne."

"To some people, kingship is a myth that was handed down to them by their ancestors."

"To other people, the candidates for the throne were not people they wanted to challenge."

"In order to crown a king, the successful king has to be equal to another one."

"The people who plan to cause harm to the throne come from outside of the royal clan."

"We must be very careful because the person who is crowned might use war for power."

"This state has had two powerful war chiefs who fought

a civil war because their candidate was not crowned an Obi."

"It was not just rivalry between states that led to war, but private wars against neighboring people."

"An Obi is the father, priest, god, and war leader of his people, and he has power over land in the area in which he lives."

"To crown an Obi without agreeing with the rules of succession could lead to a civil war."

# CHAPTER 2

Obi Okonya II sat on his throne while his children sat at his feet and listened to his royal slaves tell stories during the resting period between the planting season and the months of harvests. It was customary that at the end of the story a proverb be spoken.

Once there was a man who wanted to become a king, but the process of the purification of the leopard's blood was not complete, and purity could not be inherited. Large sums of money had to be contributed towards the ceremony. At harvest time, the man went with his family to the farm to determine the value of his yam harvest. Everybody in the household had worked all year on the farm to give him money from their harvest so that he could "carry money for the ghosts." The annual purification ceremony had to be performed to test the spiritual health of the king and the community. That night, when the birth of a soul in a new body came out into view from the bush to roam through the community, the man took down a sacred treasure box that contained the symbols of his ancestors from a shelf. The box contained four sticks that represented the ancestors, kola nuts, his personal treasures, and other valuable personal items. The man sat down on a leopard skin that was given to him by a hunter who killed a leopard during a battle. The leopard was the king of the forest, and a king was the only person who was supposed to sit on it. To establish the goodwill of his ancestors, the man begged the ghosts while the ancestors listened to his words of prayer on behalf of his family.

"Chi, bless my family."
"Chi, bless my mother's family."
"Chi, bless my father's family."
"Chi, bless my mother's father's family."
"Chi, bless my father's mother's family."
"Chi, accept me as a candidate for purification."
"Chi, guide me in good health through my tasks of purification."

After begging the ghosts on behalf of his family, the man fed the ghosts yam food. He could begin carrying money for the ghosts, he could gain full purification, he could be close to powerful spirits that affect the community, and the people could identify him with them. There is an African proverb that goes, "A wise person will always find a way."

In the village of Mbubu, people lived the good life. There were celebrations throughout the community for everything with food, dancing, and drinking. When a king was crowned, there was a celebration. When a king was dethroned, there was a celebration. Anything and everything that was good or bad was celebrated so long as the ancestors participated and the deity, one's god, understood. At every New Yam Time Festival, it was the custom of the townspeople to hold a feast that was conducted by a Juju priest who was responsible for them knowing how to invoke the juju into the yams. The priest of the yam juju prepared to speak to the townspeople. At sunrise, he entered the small, dark room of the juju house to worship some wooden objects made in honor of the ancestors. There were three natives who accompanied him. They sat down in front of him and beat their sacred drums. When the drum ceremony ended, each one of the natives had to assist the Juju priest when he was ready to invoke the juju into the yams. The first native filled a pot with fish. The second native filled a pot with water. The third native filled a pot with yams. The Juju priest and the three natives worshipped over the pots to the beat of their drums.

On the following morning, the townspeople gathered together in the village ilo to hear the Juju priest make an announcement. "I am the priest of the juju and have invoked the juju into the yams. Every man, woman, and child is to meet me here on the last day of The New Yam Time Festival. No one should quarrel or act violently towards one another. This sacred time will begin today and last for the next twenty-four days to bring protection to your yam farms." The Juju priest returned to the juju house where he spent sacred time alone giving honor to Ale, the earth goddess, who told him to make a sacrifice to Ani, the owner of all the land.

On the day of The New Yam Time Festival, the Juju priest returned to the village to see if they had practiced peace and goodwill like they were supposed to. Should the peace of the Earth Mother be broken, she would not bless the ground and leave them with a poor harvest. If the peace of the Earth Mother was respected, she would bless the earth with a bountiful harvest. Every man, woman, and child who lived in the village entered the ilo for an enormous celebration before the Juju priest arrived to speak. There is an African proverb that goes, "Knowledge is like a garden. If it is not cultivated, it cannot be harvested."

Some foreigners visited a village in Africa and asked for permission to enter the principal shrine of their juju, but before they left, they removed some objects that belonged to the chief priest from the shrine. They didn't know that they had removed the most precious and treasured objects of the chief priest's ancestors. When the news that the foreigners had endangered the law and order of Oru, the land juju, they were summonsed to appear before a native court judge who ordered them to restore the cult objects back to the shrine. "I am the chief priest of the juju house. If you do as you are told, all charges will be dropped against you. You are to return back here to me in seven days."

A canoe was prepared by the chief's slaves, and the foreigners were led to the river where they got on board the canoe and paddled up a stream back to their homes. Before returning back to the chief priest, the slave told the foreigners how to be saved from the trouble that they had brought upon themselves. "Offer a sacrifice of thanksgiving to the juju of the chief priest before you return the cult objects," and he left them standing on the bank of the Niger River. Before the foreigners arrived home safely, they were captured by a family of seven juju spirits who came up out of the river and made them their slaves.

"Who are you?"

"We removed some cult objects of worship that were in the juju house of the chief priest."

"We have seven days to report back to him or we will be charged with stealing."

"We were on our way back to the shrine when you showed up."

"Who are you?"

"We are the ancestors of a family of juju spirits who came to this region as humans. After hundreds of years, they vanished from the face of the earth."

"Why would you go back to the shrine after all of the trouble going there has already caused you?"

"The chief priest's slave who paddled us up the stream

in a canoe told us to make a sacrifice at the shrine where we found the cult objects."

"You are free to make a sacrifice at the shrine, but now you must be captured as a payment of a fine to the Juju priest."

"You are now the slaves of the juju spirits."

"We will grant you your freedom, but you must obey our commands."

"A white ram must be offered as a sacrifice. His fleece will be given to the chief priest for a coat, and the head of the ram will be used to make the chief priest a mask. Do as you are told," and the first juju spirit disappeared.

"White fowls must be sacrificed and offered to Chi. Do as you are told," and the second juju spirit disappeared.

"The fruit of the kola trees has to be set out for ghost offerings. Do as you are told," and the third juju spirit disappeared.

"A goat must be offered as a sacrifice to the land's farm spirit. Do as you are told," and the fourth juju spirit disappeared.

"Make the chief priest a drum that he will keep in his house until the great ceremonies of the village take place. Pray that he will accept it as an offering. Do as you are told," and the fifth juju spirit disappeared.

"Go into the bush, dig clay from the earth, and shape it into a ball. Catch four fish in the stream, and set them before a clay ball like people did in the beginning when there were no jujus as an offering. Do as you are told," and the sixth juju spirit disappeared.

"Make an offering to the yam spirit to show your gratitude for the yams that you have seen grow from the earth. Do as you are told," and the seventh juju spirit disappeared.

The foreigners made the seven sacrificial offerings as

they were commanded by the juju spirits, and returned to the shrine of the chief priest with the cult objects they had removed seven days ago. The priest was waiting for them inside of the house and said, "Lay the objects alongside of the shrine. Go back home, and look for a sign from Chi that you have been forgiven for breaking the law."

The next morning, the foreigners went out into the fields to inspect their crops. They found more yams than they had ever seen in all of the years before this harvest. Everything that they had planted in the spring was growing like it was supposed to, and Chi had forgiven them. There is an African proverb that goes, "He who does not look ahead always remains behind."

One day, an elephant, a giraffe, a lion, a leopard, and an ostrich roamed about the compound. They met one another and began imitating the tribes of northern and southern Nigeria. Late that night, a message from the sounds of drums could be heard throughout the village. When friends meet, it calls for a ceremony. The animals were to meet again in the compound the next day, so at cock-crow, the elephant, giraffe, lion, leopard, and the ostrich gathered together in the compound.

"Misfortune has fallen upon the village," the elephant said.

"I believe that one of the customs of the people has not been honored," the giraffe said.

"Nobody can return to their homes until the misfortune has passed," the lion said.

"They cannot be a member of their own clan," the leopard said.

"There will be no peace among the clansmen until the custom is honored," the ostrich said.

"You are all correct," the elephant said, "let's go home and meet here again in seven days."

On the seventh day of the week, the elephant, giraffe, lion, leopard, and ostrich gathered together again in the compound. A group of men and women were there having a ceremony to renew their friendships with one another. The women knelt down as they greeted one another. The men were shaking hands with one another and at the same time laying their hands over their hearts. There is an African proverb that goes, "Leave bad things, talk peace."

Once there was a child who had a troublesome spirit called Uke that was associated with misfortune. The Uke heard about the child and returned to the world as one of the child's ancestors to be with him. The Uke sent for all of the ancestors of the child's family, called the "collective reincarnate" – they could return to life or revisit the world. One night before bedtime, the child's mother said, "Since you won't obey me, perhaps you will obey the Ulaga," a figure with the head of a bird with a long head, the body of a crocodile, and the legs of a bird that are covered with cloth tights. While the child was in a deep sleep, the Ulaga ran gracefully about the room cracking a whip causing the child to wake up.

"This is for the "children of the square" whose trouble is obeying their parents," the Ulaga said, and ran and ran around the room cracking the whip and yelling at the same time.

"Stop, stop," the child said.

"I promise to stop cracking the whip when you do something that represents a commitment to one's personal god in life. I want you to tell all of your friends that the Uke will cause them great trouble if they don't obey their parents, the Uke will cause night ghosts to come from the bush and grasslands at harvest season, the night ghosts will wander through the town at night, the night ghosts will sing mysterious songs throughout the village, and they go in and out of people's houses like trick-or-treaters at Halloween."

"I promise that I will tell all of my friends my age what you have told me to tell them," the child said.

When the child obeyed the Ulaga, he was rewarded with a "children of the year" festival in the village square. There is an African proverb that goes, "A child's face is his mirror."

One morning, an Obi took down his sacred treasure box, opened it, and removed the symbols of his ancestors, a boat-like vessel made out of kola wood that was carved with white chalk to represent a white god as the ancestral ghosts and some kola nuts before he carried them with him to the shrine of past Obis. When he returned, he beat on his royal ufie drum to call upon his cabinet of chiefs, titled men, fortune-tellers, diviners, priests, and the rich people and their supporters to a meeting at his Royal Palace. He sat on his throne, a stool carved out of wood, and said, "I am to appear majestic to the community in seven days, but I need your support. I expect each one of you to visit the ancestral shrine to seek spiritual guidance for me and return here to my throne."

For every day of the week, the Obi sent each one of the seven groups of people to the ancestral shrine of the land to take communion with the spirits of the ancestors. After communion, the chiefs told the king to tell the community that he was responsible for the spiritual forces which brought him to power. After communion, the titled men told the king to tell the community that he was responsible for the superhuman ideas which brought him to power. After communion, the fortune-tellers told the king to tell the community that he gets his power from god. After communion, the diviners told the king to tell the community that he had the ability to transfer his power to his chiefs, titled men, fortune-tellers, diviners, priests, and the rich and their supporters. After communion, the priests told the king to tell the community that he had the power to send forth ghosts to make important decisions for him. After communion, the rich people and their supporters told the king to tell the community that the king never dies.

During the worship service, the chiefs, titled men, fortune-tellers, diviners, priests, and the rich people and their supporters heard the sounds of cannon shots in a distance to announce that the Obi had passed away. They joined the community in a praise song.

"Igwe eji!" "The iron is broken."
"Igwe eji!" "The iron is broken."
"Igwe eji!" "The iron is broken."

For the next twenty-one days, there was a public ceremony that began with the king's royal ufie drum beaten every morning to honor him, his family, and his friends as the community danced to express how much they appreciated him, then a communal meal was served. When his spirit departed to another world where it would join the other Obis from the past, people returned to the shrines of past Obis and poured libations, pouring a liquid as a sacrifice to god. "We make this offering of kola nuts and palm-oil for the success of the home-going ceremony of our Obi, for Obis of the past, and future Obis," the community said. There was a private ceremony for the chiefs, titled men, fortune-tellers, diviners, priests, and the rich people and their supporters. He was given a secret burial when the celebration was over. Three years later, the Obi appeared. There is an African proverb that goes, "Be glad you are unknown, for when you are known, you would wish you weren't."

# CHAPTER 3

Prince Okonya III was prepared for the challenges of the office of king, but everybody in the royal family was not convinced that he had received a good education, was knowledgeable enough about the role of an Obi, was responsible enough to hold the office, and concerned about ruling the community. The Obi's council of titled men scheduled a cabinet meeting to discuss his oral examination of the customs and traditions of kingship.

"It is unlikely for anyone to try to correct a king."

"We are trying to put an end to conflict in the community."

"We are trying to avoid jealously between clans."

"We are afraid that the dignity of Obis of the past will suffer if something is not done."

"The sacredness of the Obi could be at risk."

"It is proverbial that one does not judge the son of a king."

"A king can protect his son from judgment."

The Obi's council agreed that they would decide whether or not Prince Okonya III was qualified for a title. Each one of the titled men in their traditional dress and a red cap adorned with eagle feathers sat on a stool to ask him questions that were prepared by the oldest man on the council.

"Whose experience does an Obi rely upon to function effectively as an Obi?" the first man on the council asked.

"The titled men of the council."

"Which one of us has sat in the cabinet longer than the others?" the second man on the council asked.

"The Okpala, men whose knowledge of the customs and traditions of the community can be compared to a highly educated lawyer."

"What other reason makes an Okpala qualified to have a seat on a stool at a cabinet meeting?" the third man on the council asked.

"The Okpala should rule over the community just as a politician should, and he knows when to get involved in the affairs of the people."

"Obi Okonya II has told us that you are ready to become the next Obi. What other ways could you have become the ruler of the throne?" the fourth man on the council asked.

"A king-in-the-making can buy his title at a great price of hundreds of naira, Nigerian money, as an installment fee."

The meeting ended for a brief period to discuss his performance. When the staff of titled men agreed that Prince Okonya III had answered their questions correctly, they asked him to return to the Obi's council to finish the interview about the customs and traditions of kingship.

"Obi Okonya II has many rich relatives and friends who, if asked the question, "If somebody asked you to spend a lot of money towards the development of your community, would you say yes?" the fifth man on the council asked.

"Yes. When I become the next king I will be willing to give up my residence and move."

"What would you consider your contribution to your community as the next king?"

"I will rebuild my old residence and turn it into a civic center for the community."

"Should one of the four royal clans demand that you handle a matter of interest to them, how would you handle the matter?" the sixth man on the council asked.

"I will need their support in order to be an effective leader in the community, so such matters would have to be addressed openly before them."

"It is customary that a king comes from a royal division in most states, and in others both royal and non-royal divisions.

"When a king does not come from a royal division, what is the custom?" the seventh man on the council asked.

"The next most senior official from the non-royal division has an opportunity to contest the throne."

"Who are the members of these non-royal divisions?"

"Titled chiefs who are appointed by the Obi to perform certain functions of the government on his behalf."

The Obi's council of titled men sat together in a big circle to discuss the end of the interview. They agreed that Prince Okonya III's answers were sudden and tremendous like the last rain that came when a farmer, who was exiled from his clan, moved away to build a compound on land for a farm during the coming of the next planting season.

"We believe that his Chi has said yes."

"We should say yes also."

"The royal family will have to get over our decision."

"We are not just talking about somebody who is prepared to win a contest for the throne."

"We are talking about a prince whose forefathers were Obis."

"His whole life is ruled by a great passion to be a king."

"The community has told us nothing to cast this man

out of the Royal Palace like a fish on a beach panting for breath."

"I agree that this man's Chi has said yes."

"We have one last thing to say to you, Prince Okonya III. You are not above the law."

"You have not broken any law either."

"You are here today to be challenged by other kings, chiefs, and council members on behalf of the royal family and the community." There is an African proverb that goes, "A canoe without a steerer can easily go astray."

When Prince Okonya III was crowned Obi III, he invited a royal court made up of his kingly officials, court judges, chiefs, and any elders who wished to join him to hear the contest for the throne that was prepared for his son, Prince Ezeukwu.

"It is customary that a prince leave the Royal Palace to complete an apprenticeship."

"The king and his royal court have to decide whether or not he is responsible, honest, and mature enough to become the successor to the throne by proving his knowledge of kingship."

"It is customary that he learn about the government and administration of his own village after visiting another one."

"It is the tradition of the kingdom that the Obi is free to will the throne to any of his sons by pronouncing it so."

"Since the throne is not being inherited, the prince can live with another king and his family to get prepared for that day."

Obi Okonya III was always disappointed that Prince Ezeukwu, who was his eldest son, was not as bright as his younger brother. "My first born son is dull and slow," he would tell his fellow kinsmen. An old man who was listening said, "Have you not heard, the Obi never dies?" Obi Okonya

III had to decide who was qualified to be chosen as the heir to his throne, so his two sons had an opportunity to display their power and skill at answering questions about kingship during an oral examination. At the end of the apprenticeship, the trial began with a series of questions that were answered after the youngest son gave his answers to each question first and Prince Ezeukwu gave his answers to each question after him.

"Who is an Obi?"

"An Obi is a powerful king who is in charge of the government and administration, the customs and traditions of the people, their social and political lives, and the chief priest of the community."

"An Obi is identified with the skies, Igwe, the powerful and great one above the Obi and all mortals."

"How does a reigning king choose a successor?"

"It is the tradition of kingship that the reigning king has to choose a successor in several ways. He can tell his first-born son to succeed him, he can order his first-born son or any of his other sons to succeed him, one of his sons can inherit the throne upon the death of his father, or the customary way of all successions to the throne can be done by contest."

"The king is free to will his throne to any of his sons by simply proclaiming it. There is no definite rule for choosing the next Obi."

"If the Obi has a daughter and has no son, can she succeed him and sit on the throne?"

"It is our custom that a man in the community is always in line to be a successor on the throne if a son, brother, uncle, nephew, or any male in the family is not qualified to be an Obi."

"No. The ruler of the throne is always a man."

"What happens to the throne, should the Obi be fatherless?"

"The king is always married and has children for different reasons other than royalty."

"The Obi is unlikely to be childless because they follow our traditional religious beliefs."

"Who takes charge of the throne upon the death of the Obi when his heir is not mature enough to inherit the throne?"

"If the oldest man in the family is willing to hold the seat of Obi, the throne becomes his, but if the oldest man declines the seat of Obi, the next man in line takes control."

"A male relative holds the throne until the young prince has grown up to maturity."

"Do you fully understand why apprenticeship and training are necessary before you become the next Obi?"

"To understand the art of government and administration."

"To get prepared to succeed the king when the day comes for a new Obi."

"We have one last question before the final stage of the oral contest about kingship."

"How is the sacredness of kings expressed?"

"The kings sacredness is expressed in those rituals that send his soul to the other world to live."

"To say that a king is sacred is not true. He is only considered to be sacred, so the rules of the law are for kings and all people and should be treated as such."

The next day, Obi Okonya III challenged Prince Ezeukwu to an oral examination without his younger brother. As many who could gather together in the village ilo stood before them.

"What is the rule for choosing the next Obi?"

"There is no definite rule for choosing the Obi."

"In the past, kings can be supplied from a royal dynasty or a non-royal dynasty. In the period of contest for succession, who does the throne belong to?"

"The throne belongs to those who are the true sons of the past Obi."

"How does the royal dynasty become more powerful than the non-royal dynasty?"

"According to tradition, the office of the Obi in the royal division of the dynasty is above the office of the non-royal dynasty. They are second-class chiefs."

Obi Okonya III pulled out a book of the administrative offices that had been held by the past eighteen Obis and the members of the royal houses and asked Prince Ezeukwu questions from it.

"What is the role of an Obi?"

"The role of the Obi is to be the traditional pillar upon which rest the people of the town."

"How was the Obi brought to the throne?"

"The most powerful of the two dynasties controlled the succession to the office of the king."

"Does a candidate to the throne have to be a member of a dynasty?"

"No. Years ago, one of the dynasties supplied a "good candidate" to the throne who was a Christian, a follower of the Catholic missionaries."

"What is the custom for choosing an Obi when there are several people competing for the title?"

"The members of the Obi's council choose a candidate and present him to the chiefs. The chiefs present the candidate to all of the political divisions of the state, then they present the candidate with a gift."

"What happens when the candidate accepts the gift?"

"Once the candidate accepts the gift, the candidate

becomes the next Obi, and he is introduced to the community."

"Who has the right to choose a candidate?"

"The members of the royal dynasties clan have the collective right to determine who the candidate should be."

"What happens when more than one royal dynasty decides to supply his own candidate to become an Obi and that candidate is not supported by his dynasty?"

"A representative in the Obi's council would address the issue before the community to see to it that the candidate is appointed to the office of Obi, but the Obi has to agree to sign a written statement before being supported."

"What is the rule of holding an office?"

"The six offices of the political divisions of each state are to be held according to our ancient rules."

"Should the Obi have the power to make decisions in matters that affect the welfare and ruling of the community?"

"The Obi never makes decisions in any matter that affects the welfare and ruling of the community, but should consult with chiefs and elders first."

"Who has the right to crown an Obi?"

"The prime minister and chiefs have the right to crown an Obi."

"Who should perform the ceremony?"

"The people want a person who knows how to perform the ceremony at the Udo, a ritual at a shrine where the Obi communicates with the ancestral spirits of past Obis."

"What else is expected of the next king-in-the-making?"

"He has to learn the duties of kingship, offer sacrifices to the ancestors, and how to become a titled priest of the Udo."

"Is anybody else qualified to perform the ceremony?"

"There are other people who feel that it should be a person who has taken the Ozo title."

"What is the right place to hold the ritual?"

"The right place to hold the ritual is at the shrines of the ancestors, just so there is an ant-hill through which the candidate can become inspired by the spirits which haunt ant-hills."

"What is to be used as the emblem in association with rituals at the shrine?"

"The ofo."

"Should the candidate for king who performs the ritual sacrifice to the ancestors be a family member of the ancestors?"

"He must be a member of the same direct blood-line of the ancestor in order to perform the ritual."

In late January, a series of rituals were always performed to remove the pollution of the year, so the royal ufie drum announced the time for the first major ritual of the new season, "It is time for giving homage to the yam spirit," a spirit that guards over the yams, and it had to be worshipped each year on the farmland before it was cleared and cultivated from late January through March. During these months, each man, woman, and child met at the barn after the farmland had been cleared to worship the yam spirits which were represented by farming tools, a live cock, seeds, yams, or sticks. First, the yam spirits were fed, then somebody had to take down a sacred treasure box from a shelf and fill it with kola nuts, ancestral treasures, and symbols of the collective ancestors, the named, the unnamed, the remembered and the forgotten, and wooden objects carved from an apple tree, and the community walked together to the ancestral shrine at the Niger River. When they reached the river, the chief priests poured libations and called out the names of the ancestors in a long prayer to the yam spirit for their support throughout the planting season.

"Chi, we pray for the earth."
"Chi, we pray for the farming tools."
"Chi, we pray for the farmers."
"Chi, we pray for the yam seeds."
"Chi, we pray for health and wealth."
"Chi, we pray for our men, women, and children."
"Chi, we pray for a greater harvest this year than the year before."
"Chi, we pray for the contents of the sacred treasure box so that we may all "wash our hands" and become cool."

The king opened the sacred treasure box, reached for a bowl of water that came from the Niger River and washed his hands before he sprinkled water over the symbols of the ancestors that had been placed on the ground. He broke kola nuts, divided them, dropped pieces of the kola on the altar, took a piece for himself, handed the rest of it to his servants, distributed it to all persons who were present until it ran out, and the community ate yams. Sometimes palm-oil was poured over the objects when it was available, then one last prayer was said.

"Chi, we pray that you accept this offering."

Some of the objects that were in the sacred treasure box and yams were placed on the ancestral shrine so that everybody would know that the yam spirit ritual had come to an end. On the same day, the women prepared food for people and sent out as many plates of yams as they could. They prayed to the ancestors, covered the plates with yams when they returned back home, and listened to folktales.

One of them was about a man who would not honor an old African tradition called "bringing in his father" or "begging ghosts" to receive something from them. There was a priest who carried around a staff, a stick that was about four feet long with iron rings, that jingled when the staff is stamped on the ground. It was used like an ofo. One day the priest held his staff in his right hand and stamped it on the ground. The iron rings jingled so loud, all of the ancestors in the land could hear it as clearly as they heard its message and the ghosts appeared. The priest pleaded to the ghosts, "I want to act as a priest for the ghosts so that I may bring in my father." One of the ghosts answered, "Only a person who has spiritually been reborn in purity can act as their priest. Bring me an object of pureness that represents your father's heritage. Once you have heard from one of us, you will be the next priest of the ancestral land," and the ghosts returned to the shrines.

The priest went to his father's ancestral house to look for an object of pureness, so that the ghosts would let him "bring in his father" and let him act as priest of the ancestral land. He discovered some of the different colored pieces of cloth in a treasure box that was among some of his fathers most valued emblems of his ancestral house. The long process of ceremonial acts to beg the ghosts began. The priest raised a piece of red cloth from the treasure box and stamped the staff on the ground to call on the ghosts, but they did not answer. The priest raised a piece of black cloth from the treasure box and stamped the staff on the ground to call on the ghosts, but they did not answer. The priest raised a piece of green cloth from the treasure box and stamped the staff on the ground to call on the ghosts, but they did not answer. There was one last piece of cloth left in the treasure box, a white one. The priest raised the white piece of cloth from the treasure box, and the ghosts appeared. The priest examined the piece of white cloth and said of the priest's father, "His clothes were white, they were clean, they were a symbol of pureness, so he is a man of peace and not war." The cloth was a symbol of something that could not be inherited and that was personal purity that you obtained by completing the ceremonial acts that have been asked of you. The final step in becoming a priest for the ghost was to dress up in white, and cover your body from head to toe with white clay to appear as the ancestors did. The priest obeyed the ghost's commands, and from that day forward he had the right to act as priest over the ghosts, his father's ancestral house, the shrines, and the land.

There was a king from the western side of Iboland who always brought hundreds of slaves with him to the eastern side of Iboland every year. Upon his arrival one morning, he was well received by the beating of the royal ufie drum that sounded like it was waking up the entire community at the beginning of daylight. The chief welcomed the king and his slaves with a kola nut ceremony. After the kola nut was eaten, the talk opened.

"I have come to you today for your advice. In my land, a king is above a chief. The king does not weep for he is above ordinary men. The king does not get angry. The king does not feel sorrow. These are emotions that belong to mortal men. We have personal servants to express such feelings on our behalf. Something else that a king cannot do is make contact with cult slaves. Such spirits linger about the spirit shrines of the community, but none of them can tell me where to find my son," the king said to the chief.

"I am afraid that your son has run away and is hiding in one of the spirit groves," the chief said to the king.

"I need you to help me find out if my son has become a slave to one of the spirits of the shrines. Since we know that cult slaves, who are dedicated enough to the spirits, live in the groves of the spirit, we should take a trip to the shrine to consult with the Udo priest to find out where he is."

The king and the chief began searching along the banks of the Niger River, its lakes and streams, the ancestral shrines, every open market, mud-thatched roof huts, every ceremony, festival, feast and banquet, the rainforests, the yam fields, the villages and village squares, compounds, and neighboring towns until they reached the "Road of Slaves" where chiefs participated in slave trade between communities when it was not conducted in open market squares and the ancestral houses of chiefs, then the chief led the king to the Udo shrine where he could communicate with the Udo priest who said, "You have eaten kola from the chief's hand. Now you have to gather together a collection of sacred objects. Once you have the sacred objects, return here to me." The king went back home for seven days and returned to the Udo shrine with a royal ufie drum, an ufie gong, an ofo, a goat, a mat, an iron needle, and cowries.

"Here is your collection of sacred objects," the king said to the Udo priest. "Can I have my son back?"

"Your son has become the property of this shrine. He has watched over and taken care of its sacred grove for me. According to tradition, any person who makes contact with a cult slave must himself become one."

"According to the laws of the cult slaves, my son has a right to choose between staying with you or coming with me."

"Go back home, and wait there for your son to return to you." There is an African proverb that goes, "A king's child is a slave elsewhere."

# CHAPTER 4

Obi Mberekpe was a "divine king." We lived in a Royal Palace with chambers – a part of the Royal Palace with many rooms. One of the chambers was used as a private meeting place for kings and senior chiefs, a small chamber for public meeting places, a chamber where the Obi's annual festival was held, a chamber where the Obi received visitors and had council meetings, his personal chamber for himself and members of his family, a chamber for his bodyguards, and a private chamber where he kept his Chi shrine and worshipped it. His royal household was made up of personal servants and royal servants, but his slaves lived in a nearby village. We were one of two of the biggest tribes in Iboland. One of them was the Ibo who lived on the western side of the Niger River, and the other one was the Ibo who lived on the eastern side of the Niger River. The customs and traditions of both people were so much alike that they claimed to have the same common ancestry. Although there were cultural and political differences between them, both communities called themselves Ndi-Aniocha – the land was bountiful which made it possible for agriculture to be their chief occupation. The responsibility of the land was always shared collectively among the two communities.

During the beginning of the rainy season in June, the land on the western side of Iboland where yams are cultivated was covered with water flooding their villages which forced the community to move to the nearest village on the eastern side of Iboland and return back home at the end of the rainy season in September. The eastern communities were dry all year round near the rainforest. Nine communities from the western side of Iboland had to cross the Niger River to get to the eastern side. It took about five months for yams to mature for harvest. By the time the western Ibo communities moved to the eastern side, the men went straight to work on farmland that had already been cleared the first three months of the year when yams were planted. The women worked on women's crops – cassava, cocoyams, maize, and vegetables.

It was the responsibility of the Obi to make daily offerings to the ancestors for the welfare of his community before going to work in the fields every day at noon. The ritual had to be performed at the shrine of the goddess who guards over the water which was located in the middle of the Niger River. From June to September, a ceremony was held each month for twenty-eight days to celebrate the bounty of the land. The Obi lived in seclusion, no one was allowed to see him, in his hut with his ikenga, "a spirit of good fortune," where he prayed. When he heard the royal ufie drum, he appeared and all of the members of the western community paraded to the shrine where the king had to be in spiritual communion with the Obis of the past. The king carried his ofo with him on his way to the shrine to offer the spirits of the ancestors kola nuts and palm-oil, to pray for the success of the ceremony and the eastern side of Iboland where they would be living, guidance of the ancestors, and protection from any unknown enemies that he might have.

The Feast of The New Yam Festival was over, and it was the beginning of the dry season. It was a time for idleness, play, celebrations, warfare, the preparation for the end of the year, and the beginning of another one. It was during this season that stories were always told. The boys were encouraged to sit in the compound with the men who told them stories of the land – masculine stories of tribal warfare. The women told stories before they left home for the community square where the women held their markets every day.

The queen's council and the women's trade organization controlled the activities in the great markets. There was another organization of women who had the same function of a king, and they were called queens. There was a king called "rock which stems the flow of the great river," who was connected to powerful spirits. It was said that by day the queen and her councillors sat on their market stools near the sacred grove and supervised trade, but by night they adopted the forms of birds and gathered together in the trees of the sacred groves to talk.

Today was the most important great waterside market day held alongside the bank of the Niger River. The sacred grove was located east of the market and in the sacred grove stood a shrine. Years ago, one of the queens planted a "great ebenebe tree" near the sacred grove. The kings controlled the shrines near the great waterside market. An elder once said, "Whenever people act on an intervillage level, the likelihood that abomominations would be publicly proclaimed increased."

The abomination happened underneath the "great ebenebe tree." In the past, the king's slaves, senior chiefs, senior trading women, queens, and any outsiders aside from the kings themselves and their wives could participate in trade, but on that particular day, somebody entered the community square and violated the tradition of "covering the canoe." One of the traders reported the problem to one of the chiefs, and the chief went directly to the king. When the king heard there was a violation of their tradition in the marketplace, he made arrangements to have a ceremony to get rid of any evil spirits that might be lurking throughout the community. Chiefs, women traders, and slaves could not invade the market. The ceremony was supposed to be a tribute to the tradition of "covering the canoe," but in the meantime, he had to find a way to bring honor to the marketplace. He called upon one of the queens.

"Make a bonfire on Ibo Road. Take the burning firebrands, and wave them about your households and compounds to protect the community from evil, then return back here to me," the king said to the queen. The queen did as she was told and returned to the king.

"The path leading to Ibo Road was blocked by a woman who was "Okposi-eke," she was capable of transforming herself into various large and dangerous animals. I was afraid of her, so I ran away," the queen said.

"Carry the burning firebrands towards the Niger River past the great market, and throw them into the river to "quench the fires" of abomination, then return back here to me," the king said. The queen did as she was told and returned to the king.

"I waited and I waited for the fire in the firebrands to go out in the water, but they would not," the queen said.

"There is a powerful medicine that was buried beneath the "great ebenebe tree" by the ancient mothers of Iboland. Bring the medicine to me," the king said. The queen did as she was told and returned to the king.

"The bees in the tree raged out at me so I ran away," the queen said. "I did not get the powerful medicine."

"Very well. I will consult with the Oracle of the Hills and the Caves to find out what should happen next," the king said. The queen spent the next three days in the marketplace and at meetings. For the first time in three nights, the queen had her own idea about saving the community after a spirit came to her in a dream and said, "Go back to Ibo Road, and make a sacrifice to drive evil from the town." When the queen returned to Ibo Road, the woman who was "Okposi-eke" appeared. It was market day, and the woman had to tempt people to come into her path with her magic fan instead of frightening them away.

"Come here!" the woman said to the queen. "I want to know why you have come to the great market."

"The king sent me here three days ago because there has been an abomination in the village."

"After you left, I waved my magic fan so that you would hear from me in your dreams. How can I help you?"

"The spirits in my dreams asked me to take charge of sacrifices driving evil from the town. I have made every sacrifice that was told to me by the king, but they failed."

"I am the daughter of a tiny clan that is well-known for its native doctors. We have magic, but the secret to it working is that both of us must make a collective sacrifice in order for it to protect you." The queen and the woman walked towards the northwestern bush to the protective spirit shrine called "old woman" that was on the eastern outskirts along Ibo Road. The shrine was supposed to be served by a woman. The queen made an offering of kola nuts. The woman made an offering of chalk. They prayed to their ikenga and to the ancestral kings.

"Ikenga, we pray on behalf of the king who has sent me here."

"Ikenga, we pray for this prophet who has come to me to make an offering of kola nuts."

"Ikenga, we pray that this offering will protect my village from danger."

"Ikenga, we pray that this offering will protect her community from evil."

"Ikenga, we pray that the power of the medicine that is buried on this land will drive away witches haunting the sacred groves of the village squares by night."

A cannon was fired to announce the arrival of the queen at the king's Royal Palace the next day. The king's royal dancers performed as the royal ufie drum recalled the heroic deeds of the queen at the great market. She entered the royal square with her council of women and trade organization surrounding her. The drummers stopped playing the royal ufie drum as the king appeared to welcome the queen. He presented her with ivory bracelets, anklets, white cloth, a ceremonial sword like that of a king, a leather fan symbolizing peace, a set of drums, her own palace, gifts for her at the marketplace, a market throne, a market stool, and her own slaves for her acts of bravery. There is an African proverb that goes, "One woman can change anything, many women can change everything."

There was a king who was so wealthy he could give away barns full of yams at the Royal Palace when the first harvest ended in July. Titled men were praising harvested corn and yams before the king. Chiefs were performing their war-like dances to the beat of royal war drums, then the king fed them pounded corn in their hands because his responsibility was to see to it that his people were fed by the greatest men in the village. The chiefs took home great heaps of food and palm-oil as a reward for their dancing at the end of the celebration. The king retired to his private royal chamber where he spent weeks in communion with the spirits of the ancestors. After that waiting period came to an end, the king sent for his slaves to visit all of the chief's houses to bring them to the Royal Palace to participate in a ritual to give him strength as a powerful warrior. The slaves poured libations as the chiefs honored the king's request.

"We have come here today to bow down before you," one chief said.

"There is a special doctor at the shrine of the ancestors who has a medicine that is supposed to be smeared over the yams to give you power," another chief said.

"The next time you fall asleep, dream about all of the burdens in the community in the past year and your good fortune in the upcoming year. When you wake up from the dream, you will be filled with power," another chief said.

"Dance before the people in the villages to prove that you have strength," another chief said.

"Go to the shrine of the ancestors and commune with the great god, the land, other great spirits, and the ghosts of former kings in order to become a fierce warrior," another chief said.

The king left the Royal Palace with his servants who carried chalk and food to the riverside to feed the spirits. When the spirits are not fed, they send disease and disaster throughout the village. The feast began with feeding them roasted yams. All of a sudden, a pile of earth that was so high the king's personal servants who stood across from him could not see what was happening on the other side of the shrine came up out of the ground. He took a piece of the earth in his hand.

"Chi, drive away any evil that is stopping me from becoming a fierce, strong, powerful warrior."

"Chi, we thank you for the successful completion of this year's yam season."

"Chi, we beg you for a bountiful harvest next year."

"Chi, make our yams safe for eating."

"Chi, drive away disease and disaster from this village."

"Chi, let money and children come into my house."

"Chi, guide us back safely from this place to the next one."

"Chi, give me the strength of a powerful warrior after this ritual."

When the king was gone from the Royal Palace, his personal servant and slaves decorated his throne, sent out messages on royal war drums to everybody in the villages about his power, and called them to attend a huge festival when he returned. After a week of communion at the shrine with the great god, the land, other great spirits, and the ghosts of former kings, the king was carried into the Royal Palace by his subjects dressed in a leopard skin costume and a great headress made out of feathers. Everybody wore their finest clothes. Women wore white and ivory jewelry, the men wore white and carried ivory-tusk horns, and wore feathered caps. Men, women, and children danced around the king in the palace square singing praises to him, his chiefs, and titled men who saluted him as his personal servants sat him down on his throne before a feast of yams.

"Bring me my doctors, diviners, and members of the clan," the king said.

The doctor smeared the medicine over the yams to make them safe for eating. On the first day of the ceremony, the diviners ate roasted yams with fish, palm-oil, and a fowl. On the second day of the ceremony, the members of the royal clan ate roasted yams with fish, palm-oil, and a fowl. On the third day of the ceremony, his household ate roasted yams with fish, palm-oil, and a fowl. On the fourth day of the ceremony, the community ate roasted yams with fish, palm-oil, and a fowl. On the fifth day of the ceremony, the king ate roasted yams, fish, palm-oil, and a fowl. On the sixth day of the ceremony, the king ordered his personal servants to send for his diviners to pray. On the seventh day of the ceremony, the king retired to his private royal chamber for their answer, then the king had to carry a weight of earth on his back to prove that he had the ability to bear the burdens of power.

Once upon a time, all the birds were invited to a feast in the sky. They were very happy and began to prepare themselves for the great day. They rubbed their bodies with the symbols of Obumo, the thunder deity, with red-wood, yellow-wood, green-wood, and orange-wood dye.

"Can I go with you to the feast in the sky?" Tortoise asked the birds.

"We know you are skillful at playing tricks," one of the birds said.

"You can come with us," said another bird to Tortoise, "but you must promise to leave your mischief here."

"In case you haven't heard about me, I have changed and will keep my promise to be grateful for the invitation to go with you," Tortoise said

"You have no wings to fly," the birds laughed.

Each one of the birds gave Tortoise a feather until he had enough to fly with them. When the guests arrived at the party, they were greeted with kola nuts before a feast of yam soup with fish, goat meat, vegetables, and palm-oil. Tortoise was the first one to eat, and he ate the best part of the soup and drank most of the palm-oil. The birds flew home on an empty stomach and took the tortoise's feathers with them. Obumo, who had been watching from his home in the clouds, came to his rescue.

"Don't tell me you broke your promise not to be mischievous," he thundered at Tortoise.

Tortoise tucked his head into his shell that had filled out with food and drink and thought about the bad deed he had done. "If the load is too heavy for someone to carry, one would be better off to give the load to the ground to carry," Obumo said.

Court hearings were always held in the Royal Palace before an Obi. The court of a kingly official, the members of the family, the head of the court, the elders, the judges, or anyone who cared to be present were there. One day, Obi Mberekpe was summonsed to appear as a member of the supreme court to listen to conflicts concerning two arguments – one was over whether or not a chief from the eastern side of Iboland should continue to be the king of the western side of Iboland, and the other one was a disagreement about land. All parties were given an opportunity to show their might.

"Have the fees been paid for this hearing?" the judge asked.

"I have paid two shillings and a bottle of palm-oil to bring this hearing before the court," the king said.

"We are here to settle both arguments and I am ready to hear the charges that have been brought before me," the judge said.

"Is it possible for powerful chiefs to challenge an Obi?"

"He can be challenged by his chiefs or an individual."

"The king is sacred."

"He is not above the law."

"We are here to ask that you rule this man's position of king unconstitutional."

"Is it customary to remove a person from a position such as an Obi?"

"No."

"What do you suggest we do?"

"There are rumors about people who are planning to remove the Obi from his office by giving him an assignment that is impossible for him like bringing an alligator pepper from the Niger River that had dropped out of the king's mouth, or stop a tree that had been cut down from falling, or cover a hole with a mat underneath his chair so that he would fall in it."

"The constitution states that an Obi can be removed by the Obi's council."

"My community wants to offer you a gift as a settlement for you to volunteer to step down from the throne."

"These people have placed the title of Obi on a person who is not qualified to be a king."

"The people have brought this charge to your attention because there is conflict in the community about his appointment."

"On behalf of the community, the court would like to hear from the Obi."

"We would classify the Obi's action as a threat to the welfare of the community."

"He is stirring up a rebellion that may lead to the loss of the throne if he doesn't step down."

"This act has affected the feelings of the people in a way that the community has decided not to support him, the Obi's council, or the government."

"Any act that is dangerous or threatens the well-being of the community can lead to the removal of the Obi."

"We are here to try to determine a solution to this problem."

"On the eastern side of Iboland, there are no kings."

"The crowning of a king who is from the eastern side of Iboland is considered to be a violation of the role of the royal dynasty when that king moves to the western side of Iboland."

"I am a descendant of the clansmen from the western side of Iboland."

"We, the members of the Obi's council, find such action improper, but subject to a fine and not dethroning."

"He believed that he belonged to the royal lineage when he contested the throne."

"He thought that he had a right to compete for political office before he was crowned."

"This man has a lawful right to the throne."

"He can be considered an adopted member of the royal dynasty."

"The Obi is a superior position and the chief is his servant and advisor."

"The office of king is not reserved for persons from your dynasty."

"Because this man was a chief, he is not able to answer the Obi's summons to attend meetings in the palace."

"The title has been granted to a person not ritually qualified for it."

"There are certain societies that an Obi has to be a member of, or he would be considered "bu onu ofo," he has no respect for his father."

"The ancestral ceremony has not been performed for him to be considered a part of their union, fraternity, and council."

"The kingmaker administers an oath to the Obi to pay back any money he has borrowed while he is in office."

"To carry such money with you to the throne would be a disgrace to the position of Obi."

"What are your other charges against this man?" the judge asked.

"The western community that moved to the eastern side of Iboland had their own land that was used for farming."

"The priest of the eastern part of the land performed the rituals necessary for the leasing of the land."

"The western community decided to declare the farmland residential land and create a township."

"A land committee, the Obi's council, and the Obi agreed to have this land used for the purpose of a township."

"They signed the lease on behalf of the western community."

"After several years of the development of the township, their neighboring village community from the eastern side of the community claimed that the land that was leased to the western community belonged to them."

"That is the reason why we have brought the case before the native court."

"The priests of the land have not performed the rituals necessary for the leasing of the residential land, farmland, and communal land."

"A neighboring village has claimed that part of the communal land belonged to them."

"The charge is what part of the land belongs to the village?"

"Money that is yours is not a loss once one knows the person they are supposed to pay back."

"This Obi must be dethroned to keep in touch with our history."

"This Obi is a king of the government's choice, not the people."

"An Obi who has not paid money back to the person he borrowed it from might be attacked by one of the ancestral spirits that visit the family of those people."

"There are deities connected with kingship that are powerful and the visits that are being discussed."

"You have no proof that this Obi owes money to anybody."

"One of the women's associations trusted him enough to give money to him."

"He has not refused to return the money that was given to him by the association."

"The act that he committed is considered to be a private matter."

"These people have brought the land case against me to force me to resign as Obi. The community assembled at the Royal Palace, selected the candidate of their chioce, and I was crowned. You have heard nothing here today to suggest that I cannot remain a king."

"I want the Obis from the western side of Iboland and the chiefs from the eastern side of Iboland to leave the court. When the judges are ready to tell you what we have to say about this matter, you will be asked to return," the judge said.

"A king is not a person who is a ruler with absolute power and authority."

"He reigns over a kingdom."

"The constitution states the rules of conduct of the king."

"The Obi who crowned the chief took the oath of office, and he promised to rule the land."

"Part of the oath was to consult with chiefs before making important decisions."

"Another important oath of office is to rule wisely."

"The Obi has a right to appoint who he desires to the highest senior official from any division."

"That official is not a king."

"The Ibo on the eastern side of Iboland have no king."

"This chief is only eligible to rule his community on the eastern side of Iboland."

"We have tried to show you here in this case that the violation of these rules should lead to his dethronement."

"The Obis of the western side of Iboland can appoint kings and chiefs."

"The people who live on the eastern side of Iboland can only appoint chiefs."

"If a chief is wealthy enough, the Obi's council can appoint him to be a kingly chief."

"In some states, the position of the king is weak compared to the chiefs."

"Both kings and chiefs are required to obey the rules of the constitution."

"The kings in their coronation rituals are made to take the oath of office as well as any other office."

"The kings must obey the rules of the constitution."

"The kings rule the people."

"The kings and chiefs in all states are expected to serve the interests of their people."

"The chief has a right to withdraw his support of his title by boycotting his position."

"The boycott has to be done by a group and not the chief."

"This is not a matter concerning which side of Iboland a king should be crowned."

"I am here today to avoid a civil war because of the choice of candidates."

"The judges of this court will give you an answer when we return."

"This trial reminds me of some men who wanted to become kings."

The drums beat, the flutes sang, and the spectators held their breath as the ekwe, a wooden drum, could be heard throughout the village. The community was possessed by the spirits of the drums. A man who wanted to become a king had to first take the Igbu title. Fees had to be paid to become a member, and fees had to be paid to "feast the members." The Obis-to-be were called to the throne to show proof of their interest in becoming the next Obi. The candidates paraded to the ancestral shrine to find out what they could present to the king for their title. The bell man walked in front of the three candidates jingling the "Mbgilifba imi na anya," the bell with human features to notify the priest of the ancestral shrine that the Obis-to-be were coming. Each one of them prayed for help to become a titled man.

"Ikenga, bless me with heroism," the first candidate said.

"Ikenga, bless me with income," the second candidate said.

"Ikenga, bless me with animals," the third candidate said.

The three candidates for a title walked back to the Royal Palace where the Obi asked each one of them to make their offer to become a king. The Obi asked the first candidate to make his offer to become a king.

"Do you have the whole leopard, do you have any part of the leopard, have you purchased the leopard, or have you buried the leopard?"

"I have the leopard's claws, teeth, and skin," the first candidate answered.

"That offer is worth 3,000 naira," the Obi said.

The Obi asked the second candidate to make his offer to become a king.

"I bring you seven fishing ponds. The public can go and fish in these ponds, sell the fish, and the money can be given to you. After the flood season, we will make your gift an annual celebration that will be shared throughout the community," the second candidate answered.

"That offer is worth 7,000 naira," the Obi said.

The Obi asked the third candidate to make his offer to become a king.

"I have a goat, a bullock, a fowl, kola nuts, and palm-oil for ritual ceremonies at the ancestral shrines of the land," the third candidate answered.

"That offer is worth 5,000 naira," the Obi said.

"The candidate with the most naira is the winner," and the title went to the second candidate. There is an African proverb that goes, "A tree is known by its fruit."

After several hours, the judge returned before the supreme court to determine the end of the trial.

"The traditions that you speak of have been handed down through the ages and are no longer the laws of the land."

"When the customs and traditions of a people are, the Ibo have no king, it could lead to the dethroning of that king."

"When the people believe that a person's actions are a threat to their property, which is the land disagreement, it could lead to the dethroning of a king."

"Actions that affect the feelings of the people can lead to the loss of support from the community."

"Actions that threaten the physical well-being of the people could lead to the dethroning of a king."

"When you accepted the crown to become a king on the western side of Iboland when you were a chief on the eastern side of Iboland, you took a chance of losing your position of Obi."

"The position of Obi is sacred."

"It must be observed as sacred in the interest of the community."

"The rule of the land in this case is the title of Obi is hereditary."

"It should not be transferred to a person who is a member of the same family either."

"One does not raise himself to the status of an Obi."

"An Obi does not assume the privileges of an Obi."

"Crowning a man Obi does not make him one."

"This court is made up of judges from more than thirteen neighboring groups."

"This is a mixed court with mixed emotions about the customary rules of kingship."

"The people don't believe that this court is qualified to interpret the law."

"Some of us doubt if this court understands the issues of this trial."

"The judges of this court, and both sides of the land, ask that the people select a new candidate and crown him."

"This dispute has been settled," the judge said. "You cannot be identified with royalty, so you must retire the emblems of Obiship that have been bestowed upon you – the ofo, the royal ufie drum, the leopard skin, the sword, the crown, the robes, the eagle feathers, and the elephant tusk to this court – not because of traditions, customs, or laws, but withdraw from the throne and surrender your title in the interests of dynastic unity."

"If you are not satisfied with our decision, an appeal can be made from this court directly to the Obi's court. It can also go to the court of one of the kingly officials, to a divisional court, an intermediary court, a three-divisional court, before the ancestral shrine, the lower courts, the higher courts, or one of the native courts, then this court will hear your case again."

After the judges ruled in favor of the Obis from the western side of Iboland, the king was dethroned and the emblems of office were returned to the court. Conflict increased between the community from the western side of Iboland and the community from the eastern side of Iboland. The king was the greatest warrior of his community, and the victory he had accomplished as an Obi was celebrated throughout the village. There was never any other course of action against him other than he was dethroned, but he thought he had to flee from his clan. He had been accused of a crime against the earth goddess, and a man who committed it had no other choice. A chief and his family who go outside of their village were likely to become objects of attackers from other villages. Before the cock crowed, he and his family would be heading towards the land of his mother just beyond the borders of the village of Mbubu, a village called Mbanta. He was well received by the kinsmen in his mother's village. That night, he sat down on a goatskin rug and thought about why a man should suffer for a crime he didn't even know he had committed, but he found no answer.

The next day was not the traditional annual festival of the state to honor kings and chiefs, new members of titled associations, births or deaths, but the return of one of their sons abroad. He sat down with his family on the first day of his arrival in Mbanta and told them the full story. A part of the celebration of his return was a gift-giving ceremony. He was given a plot of ground on which to build his new compound and two or three pieces of land on which to farm during the coming planting season. From cock-crow until the chickens went to roost, the community sang and danced while the chief paid a tribute to the ancestral spirits at the shrine. While the chief worshipped at the ancestral shrines of the land, the community paid "leopard tribute" to him. The chief made his tribute at the ancestral shrine near the river to honor his homecoming. The priest of the shrine gave him the power to control the spirit shrine that lived along the Niger River called, "It eats Nri, people," which didn't really eat people, but could destroy men who misbehaved throughout the community.

When the queen of the village of Mbubu heard about

the rumors of war, she set sail for the Carribean with her royal servants to meet with the Principal Officers of the Establishment of Jamaica. She arrived with goats and sheep, a very great train of camels, mules, horses carrying spices, gold, silver, ivory, apes and peacocks, precious stones, fruits, vegetables, silk, brass, leather, garments, armour, copper, and instruments to give to them as gifts. Oil portraits of Jamaican governors and colonial heroes graced the walls of the meeting room.

"I am here to tell you what is in my heart," the queen said.

"There is not anything that I wish to hide from you."

"I have heard of all of your wisdom. Now I have come here to give you these gifts."

"Mine eyes have never seen the prosperity of your land. I have only heard of your fame."

"Is it a true report that I heard in mine own land of thy acts and of thy wisdom to wage war with the African Company?" the queen asked.

"Yes, the rumors are true."

"I believed not the words of the rumors until I came here to Jamaica to ask you."

"Mine eyes have never seen an abundance of gifts such as the ones set before me from your country."

"I will promise you a hundred and twenty more talents of gold, spices, precious stones, ivory, and silk. I will give you anything your heart desires not to go to war with the village of Mbubu."

"One half of the riches in your village are greater than your promises."

"I am ready to hear thy wisdom to do judgment and justice which god has put in your heart."

"If the Royal Jamaican Company wins the war, our

victory will be far greater than all the kings in Africa for riches and for wisdom."

"I will turn away from you and return back to Africa."

"What's got to be has got to be."

"No one is to blame."

The drums beat and the flutes sang "The Land Of The Negroes."

"Early one hot sad morning, caravans journeyed along the sea coast making their voyage towards our kingdom on the 8th of the month in August, carrying a miserable company of seamen whose eyes looked for captives in the midst of their great sorrow."

"Without understanding the words of their language, like Sodom and Gomorrah, each one fell where his lot took him parting fathers from sons, husbands from wives, brothers from brothers, sisters from sisters, and mothers from their children."

"The voices of their cries for help were like "Father of Nature" and "Mother Earth" and were loud enough to reach heaven and the custom of their country of throwing themselves on the ground."

"Their misery made me feel the energy of them clinging to one another so tight you could not separate them because their some forty souls were torn from their own flesh that morning, and I asked myself, "Are they not the generation of the sons of Adam? and "Were they not baptized as Christians?"

"I felt sorrow for the men, women, and children who were sold into slavery and taken to different districts of other continents, yet they didn't feel sorrow for themselves, but found favor with god instead. Now it was the lot of the captives and the seamen who believed that they lived without the light of the holy earth, lived like beasts, lived without reasonable customs, lived without knowledge, lived without the covering of clothes, lived without houses, and lived without understanding the difference between good and bad in their motherland which gave them an opportunity to fly."

"Seamen captured four negroes, then nine negroes, then hundreds of negroes, then thousands of negroes, then millions of negroes for a little gold dust and dared them to seek their freedom before landing in the next country."

# CHAPTER 5

On the day Obi Mberekpe returned to the Royal Palace from the court hearing, a document known as "The Establishment" was delivered to him from the Royal Jamaican Company that changed the future of the village of Mbubu. The company was organized by a group of men who called themselves the Lords Of Trade. Board members, council members, traders, merchants, planters, and trade companies gathered together at the House Of Lords to talk about some of the conflicts they were having with the sugar colonies and the African Company for negro slaves to work on the sugar plantations.

"In Jamaica, sugar is king."

"Jamaica is considered to be the most fruitful land in the Carribean."

"We are the largest world producer of sugar."

"The main occupation of the Carribean islands today is sugar."

"The sugar-cane plantations are the labor of the negro in Jamaica."

"The second occupation is negroes."

"A Jamaican sugar estate requires thousands of negroes to be productive."

"Gold, slaves, ivory, and pepper have been discovered by other nations who are exploring Africa."

"Jamaica is the main producer of pimento."

"Spices grow here in plenty and wild in the mountains."

"There are over thirty-six trade companies throughout the world who are exploring Africa."

"The Royal Jamaican Company demands ownership of the slave trade from Jamaica to Africa."

"We want ownership of the factories and forts there."

"Why is the number of factories decreasing on the continent?"

"The forts are taking the place of factories."

"It would be impossible to carry on the slave trade without the assistance and protection of its forts."

"The negroes on the West Coast are so dear to the slave traders."

"The problem here is what we can afford to pay for slaves and still make a profit."

"The plantations must have negroes to work on sugar, tobacco, indigo, and rice plantations."

"We need to develop trade in gold, ivory, beeswax, medicine, and dye."

"We need to sell the negro slaves to private traders on the coast of Africa."

"I have a grant from England for $10,000 to supply them with products and negroes over the next four years."

"We can ask for $20,000 should we need to pay any additional expenses and not a penny more."

"The first shipment of negroes from Africa to Jamaica was 300."

"Obi Mberekpe wants us to deliver 23,000 negroes to him from Jamaica over the next seven years."

"After that shipment, he wants us to deliver 39,000 negroes over the next nine years."

"The negroes carried by African vessels are of much better quality than those brought by the English."

"This company already owes money to France."

"If it is not paid, the company will have to stop doing business with them."

"This isn't a business, it is a contest."

"We have sowed the seeds for a financial disaster."

"England and France are competing with one another for the sugar islands."

"The French vessels are of better quality than those brought here by the English."

"The French pay less money for their vessels than the English do."

"The French are selling their sugar for a price that is less than the English."

"Traders are complaining that the French can sell sugar for less than the English."

"French planters can purchase negroes for less money."

"This company is paying traders in Africa a higher price for negroes."

"The French are able to set their own price."

"A strong English company can drive the French from Africa."

"That is only possible with the help from other trading companies."

"For the past ten years, my company has been doing business in the West Indies."

"A friendly chief invited the English to settle down along the coast of West Africa to build factories."

"Another chief invited the English to settle down along the coast of West Africa to build forts."

"A couple of years later, warfare between Portugal and England began."

"We want to be able to get contracts to trade in Africa without asking for them."

"Merchants have organized a committee to discuss sharing the expense of a boycott against trade companies."

"We disagree with their prices for negroes."

"We disagree with the number of negroes who should be carried on a vessel."

"We don't have enough information about trade to reach an agreement."

"The African Company is trying to send a large number of ships to trade on our territory."

"We are asking that all trade activity in the Carribean stop."

"Give the Royal Jamaican Company an opportunity to reach an agreement."

"You can renew your old contract, and we can conduct slave trade on the same territory."

"We will stop the slave trade on your territory before we agree to that."

"It is difficult to reach an agreement between the parties here."

"The fight for the control of the slave trade has continued."

"If you try once and you fail, you can always try again."

"Property that belongs to other trading companies is being taken at the ports."

"Goods that belong to other trading companies are being taken."

"The companies at the Spanish-American ports are being overpaid for negro slaves."

"More than 5,000 negro slaves were taken and resold in the past three years."

"The renewing of old contracts or new ones is not bringing about peaceful trade."

"The slave trade is growing difficult and African trade is failing."

"Half of the number of men, women, and children who are being delivered to Jamaica from Africa is not healthy."

"The trade companies of Portugal, France, Holland, Denmark, England, Germany, Italy, and Belgium continue to want to have a part of the slave trade market."

"Scandanavia, Brazil, Spanish-America, South America, Great Britain, Sweden, Cuba, and the Dutch want to have a part of the slave trade market."

"These countries not only want the power to control trade, they want to own Africa."

"They have quarreled with people in Africa for years to expand their trading forts on the West Coast."

"These companies are annoying one another in Africa and other continents."

"They are struggling to control what they are discovering in Africa."

"Their disturbances cause trouble among the African tribes."

"There is only one European nation that has ever withdrawn from conducting business on the African coast."

"We have heard that they are considering selling their establishments in Africa."

"Forts can be purchased for very little money."

"There is a company that travels to the African coast for over 1,200 negroes a year."

"It is customary to collect negroes on the islands and employ them in agriculture."

"Companies have destroyed one another's settlements in Africa."

"The priests are a dependable source of contact with the natives in Africa."

"The disagreement between them is over property rights."

"There are countries that have as many as twelve or thirteen forts conducting trade."

"Those countries are building forts in parts of Africa that are powerful enough to destroy them."

"We own several small islands that trade with the islands of other nations."

"Trade is more important to them than the business of supplying the islands they own with negro labor."

"Other countries themselves are at war with one another for negroes."

"The natives themselves respect some countries more than others."

"Other countries are clinging to Africa for negro slaves."

"It is because of the sugar industry."

"In the beginning, all the islands used slave labor on the sugar plantations."

"The money earned from the sale of sugar will pay for the cost of labor."

"The Dutch and the French want their own territory in Africa for trade."

"There is no benefit for this nation to make such an agreement."

"Africa wants to be sure that the cargoes are sold and paid for before they arrive."

"The colonists are looking to buy negroes from other islands."

"Our neighboring islands are our competitors."

"The colonists would gain power and their neighbors would become weaker."

"Africa is no longer interested in conducting business with us for its own welfare."

"These conflicts could lead to a war between the African Company and the Royal Jamaican Company."

"War between both companies will make it difficult to transport negroes to the islands."

"Some of the planters on the islands have been told that they have to get negroes wherever they can find them."

"Africa is asking for 12,000 and 15,000 pounds of sugar for every negro that is delivered to us."

"The French have captured factories for slaves in West Africa."

"They will never solve the problem of supplying slave labor."

"We are negotiating with France to start a new company to explore Africa to carry slaves to other islands."

"All of the countries are having some domestic problems."

"They think the negroes will solve their problems for them."

"A very rich Portugese merchant wants to carry 3,500 to 5,000 negroes a year into other sugar colonies."

"The Dutch Company wants to bargain with Spain for 3,000 negroes to be delivered within the next six months."

"An Italian Company is asking for us to sign a contract to deliver 400 negroes."

"The Dutch and West India Company wants 1,400 negroes."

"The Italian and the Dutch-West India Company will sell negroes to the Spaniards."

"The unlimited buying power of these countries is a gold mine to all of us."

"Thirty-five hundred negroes are being sold a year to Spain for silver."

"Our contract states that all negroes delivered to Jamaica by these companies will belong to the Spaniards."

"Contracts are being written to supply thousands of negroes from other countries."

"Jamaican planters feel very disadvantaged to trade with the Spanish for negroes."

"There has been no profit for them."

"It's never too late for a shower of rain."

"There are companies here today that have traded along the coast before slave trade began."

"The best thing in life is to be free."

"The most valuable product in demand today is gold."

"The most valuable product in demand today is negroes."

"Large numbers of negroes are being sold to the African Company that should remain on their plantations."

"The Spaniards want the West Indies to deliver 1,200 negroes to work in silver mines."

"Negroes have been exported by the companies and have not fallen into the hands of planters on the islands."

"Eighteen months ago, war broke out between two countries when a dispute for trade was not settled."

"We are still looking at the possibility of war with Iboland if this contract with Obi Mberekpe is not honored."

"Jamaica will owe millions of dollars to the African Company if the contract is not settled."

"We have considered the sale of negroes to other countries to bring money to the island."

"The idea is not going well with the planters."

"The Royal Jamaican Company should proceed with a written agreement for negroes to arrive on vessels to Iboland."

"In order to trade negroes, wouldn't it be necessary to have them?"

"Jamaica cannot afford to supply the African Company or any other company with any more negroes."

"The Royal Jamaican Company was created to be the base for the sale of negroes."

"It is January, and the king is still waiting for negroes to arrive on vessels to Iboland."

"We are creating more problems for ourselves than we can handle."

"There are problems within the organizations of the companies that we fear will lead to their failure."

"Many of the companies need more money to survive."

"We are even competing with pirates."

"The pirates are discouraging the trade that the companies want control of."

"They are troublesome on the West Coast and on the East Coast of Africa."

"The competition between traders of the nations is enough without having to compete with pirates."

"The new companies don't have experience and are not very well organized."

"Most of us are having problems hiring ships, buying goods, and recruiting men from Africa."

"The Royal Jamaican Company is involved in a disagreement with too many companies here today."

"We were promised $120,000 from Africa for gold and negroes, but we only received $60,000.

"The companies are having trouble in the plantations that used credit to get paid for slaves."

"Most of the companies are being forced to borrow money to pay the trade companies back."

"The African Company and the Royal Jamaican Company are both in danger of being destroyed."

"There is a company in Africa that wants to deliver up to 3,000 negroes to Jamaica in one year."

"We can only afford to pay for half that many."

"This island is using sugar to pay back the money that was borrowed."

"War will only add to the difficulty we are already experiencing with the slave trade."

"A war might involve half of the earth."

"We are getting ready for a holy war."

"At this point in the game, this company is going to either sink or swim."

"We ben juggling rumors of war."

"Rumors them spreading."

"Who is without fault, let him cast the first stone."

"I don't see no stone, so I know I'm not alone."

"Take the beam out your eyes before you take mine."

"Take a look into yourself, stop wasting my time."

"The Royal Jamaican Company winning a war against the other companies will depend upon the maritime people."

The drums beat and the flutes sang "The Monsters of Slavery."

"Madagascar, the fascinating, giant island nation that looks like it was washed out to sea, and separated from the crust of Africa by cyclones, is where the Nile crocodiles made their way from the continent, and pirates had their headquarters."

"This treasure is a good fortune for scientists who collect fossils of dinosaurs that are millions of years old, but the roots of the Madagascar negroes who were brought into the colony during the slave trade is still uncertain."

"The ghosts of their ancestors cross the bridges of the land and waterways that connect Madagascar and East India to haunt the monsters of the slave trade on the land that is at the end of the earth."

# CHAPTER 6

Obi Mberekpe ordered his slaves to build him a castle when he was crowned the king of the village of Mbubu. He named it The Castle of Ophra because Ophra was the site for the first settlement where the greatest part of the trade of six or seven thousand negroes a year on the "Slave Coast" took place. The castle was used as a meeting place for kings and their administrators. It was the largest and strongest castle in Africa with forts, factories, an army of one thousand slaves, and over fifty-three troops. The people who lived inside of it were natives, soldiers, writers, a chaplain, surveyors, bookkeepers, stewards, surgeons, a lieutenant, sergeants, a corporal, a drummer, carpenters, smiths, bricklayers, masons employed in building and maintenance, coopers for packing and unpacking goods, armourers for repairing weapons, and gardeners for the preparation of the food that was eaten. The king called his chief ministers, kings, the Agent-General, two hundred gromettos, castle slaves brought from other parts of Africa to work, the Court of Assistants, senior chiefs, junior chiefs, the council, slave captains, two sergeants, forty-seven soldiers, and three merchants for a kola nut ceremony. The first merchant was a gold-taker, the second merchant was a warehouse-keeper, and the third merchant was a bookkeeper. After the "kola for talk" ceremony, the kola nut was divided into parts beginning with half the total share of the kola nut to kings, three-fifths of the total share of the kola nut to senior chiefs, and three quarters of the total share of the kola nut to junior chiefs.

The bookkeeper read a document that was delivered to Obi Mberekpe from the Royal Jamaican Company. "In the name of the Lord Amen. On the 25th of January before me, We, the Lords of Trade and witnesses, and the House of Lords came and appeared under god and do hereby declare to have made this contract in the form and manner here-in-after describe the following things done in Jamaica in the presence of the House of Lords and free citizens here, acting as witnesses here-unto invited. In order to avoid future disagreement which might frustrate the Royal Jamaican Company, future plans to buy, sell, and trade negroes, the good offices of Dukes and Yorks was used to prepare this paper with the Council of Trade in Jamaica to be sent to Obi Mberekpe in Iboland on their behalf. We the members of the House of Commons after having heard all opinions from the present body hereby declare that your grievances about money, competition, and rivalry of the trade industry among other nations lead us to the decision that the following companies can no longer conduct business on the continent of Africa because they have failed to re-establish themselves as profitable and have sank under "the burden of debt." They are the James, the Carlisle, the Delight, the Margaret, the Dolphin, the Falconbergh, the Averilla, the Three Brothers, the Ann, the Maurice & George, the Angola, the Barbados Merchant, the Lords of Trade and Plantations, the Lisbon Merchant, the New River Company, the Royal Adventurers, the Royal African Company, the Swedish African Company, the English Royal African Company, the Crown, the Brazil Company, the Gambia Adventurers, the Guinea Company, the Calabar River, the Gambia River, the Gambia Adventurers, the Senegal Adventurers, the

Senegal River, the Governor and Company of Adventurers of London, the Merchant Adventurers, the Company of the West Indies, the Company of the Senegal, the Danish-West India Company, the English-West India Company, the Dutch-West India Company, the Company of the Coast of Africa, the French-Senegal Company, the Royal Company of Santo Domingo, the Royal Company of the Senegal, the Company of Royal Adventurers, and the Company of the Coast of Africa. The Deputy Governor of Jamaica is pleased to make known the grievances stated in this paper regarding trade from Jamaica to Africa, Africa to Jamaica, and the future of both companies. We the committee of the House of Commons agree to create a company that is strong enough to wage a war against the village of Mbubu in the event that the demands of this letter are not honored. The Royal Jamaican Company and the failing companies have agreed to organize a war-party with the African Company and have decided when the war will begin, how it will be fought, and how war will affect all parties involved, in the event that the following terms and conditions are not met."

1. A license be granted to companies giving them permission to trade in Africa.
2. A license be purchased at a cost of $10,000.
3. Negroes delivered to Africa from Jamaica will cost $150 each and in the next two years $155 each.
4. The length of a contract be fourteen years.
5. The negro population from the West Indies to Africa and from Africa to the West Indies be recorded.
6. The only supply of negroes taken from parts of Africa be taken from the company's territory.
7. Reduce competition between companies.

8. One company will develop the gold mines of Africa and another company will carry the gold from Africa to Jamaica.
9. The Royal Jamaican Company wants to take control of slave trade and the profits from the African Company.
10. A new administration will be established to improve the conduct of trade.
11. A committee will be responsible for the control of trade companies.
12. The buyers of negroes will take nothing except money for slaves.
13. The negroes ordered to be delivered to Africa ought to be stout and strong fellows, ready for work, and for war if it is necessary to declare war against a company.

"The document that was just read to you states the new contract for trade with the Royal Jamaican Company."

"Slave vessels could already be heading to the village of Mbubu from the West Indies."

"From April through September, the trade of negro slaves with the African Company will decrease."

"They are discouraged that the fortunes to be made from trade have not increased."

"This company is in need of money to stay in business."

"Gold is the first major product of trade, negroes, ivory, and corn are second."

"The forts are more expensive to operate now than when they were first built."

"The factories are being destroyed by the enemy and our own natives."

"We are interested in negro slaves for service positions in offices in Africa."

"We need to give up the factories because we can no longer pay employees to work in them."

"We have reduced our small crafts to three or four with twenty to thirty soldiers."

"We can hire canoes but the crews are made up of natives."

"This company is using servants to conduct castle-trade."

"Our employees are still strong in number with over three hundred white men on our staff besides castle-slaves."

"If we go to war with the Royal Jamaican Company, those numbers will decrease."

"If we go to war with the Royal Jamaican Company, the prices of negroes will increase."

"A war will stop castle-trade."

"We will need money to pay the remaining employees."

"We have enough gold to pay salaries and wages right now."

"It will be expensive to recruit men to fight a war against Jamaica."

"The cost of salaries, wages, building, maintenance, small craft, coastal communication, and trade has doubled."

"The men from the failing trade companies might help us."

"It will be very expensive to train outsiders to learn the languages of the natives, the politics of Africa, and trade."

"Life here is uncomfortable, and work is becoming harder."

"Fewer and fewer men look to Africa to make a fortune."

"We are still the main attraction of other nations throughout the world."

"In the past, the Royal Jamaican Company has conducted business satisfactorily."

"I agree with the African Company that we need to make trade easier."

"We need to give credit for power to the company that deserves it."

"We need to protect ourselves against pirates and other enemies."

"The pirates have control of the East India route to Africa."

"The worst attacks on ships at sea are caused by pirates who sail as many as seven vessels at one time."

"They are looking for other ships sailing from Jamaica to Africa and Africa to Jamaica."

"None of these companies can overpower Africa."

"Our records show that the African Company owes over $20,000 to the Royal Jamaican Company."

"Those negro slaves have already been delivered to them."

"It is the planters in the West Indies who owe money to the African Company."

"The last voyage to the West Indies carried 267 negroes and only 68 arrived alive."

"Our chief priest has told us that the number of sick negroes on vessels are affected by small-pox and starvation."

"The slave captains reported negroes being shackled together."

"We are forced to ship negroes who are twelve to forty years old."

"The buyers are not as interested in negroes after the age of thirty."

"We question the number of negroes that were supposed to have been shipped to Africa."

"The Royal Jamaican Company and the African Company have not completed their contracts."

"The merchants, planters, and traders have not completed their contracts either."

"The West Indies shipped as few as a half dozen negroes to Africa in the past year."

"The Royal Jamaican Company owes the African Company over $60,000 for sugar."

"The sugar was never received or paid for."

"The African Company owes several thousand dollars to the Royal Jamaican Company for negroes."

"Both companies owe money to the Dutch, to England, London, and other countries."

"We can still deliver negroes to the islands without going to war."

"Millions of dollars have already been lost in merchandise and slaves."

"That was on outward and homebound voyages that were never delivered."

"The African Company has been in business for over eighty years shipping goods throughout the world."

"The value of the shipment is worth millions of dollars."

"It has also sent hundreds of ships to Jamaica and delivered thousands of negro slaves to their sugar plantations."

"It also bought thousands of tons of sugar from Jamaica and built forts and factories along the African coast."

"The Jamaicans created the first company to voyage from London to Africa and back to the West Indies."

"Our goal was to deliver sugar and collect negro slaves, gold, silver, ivory, wax, dyewood, hides, and gum."

"Our records show that they have not paid us over $300,000."

"In one year, over fifty ships sailed to and from Africa."

"The James, the Carlisle, the Delight, the Margaret, the Dolphin, the Falconbergh, the Averillo, the Three Brothers, the Ann, the Elizabeth, the Maurice and George, and the Angola are some of the most powerful ships."

"Most of the other ships never returned because they were lost at sea and unseaworthy."

"Other ships were unprepared for attacks and taken by the enemy."

"Bad seamanship is another problem."

"The ships sail in bad weather and meet hurricanes forcing them to return to the West Indies."

"Some ships have met an earthquake in Jamaica."

"We are failing."

"Where is our money for the work we have done for over a century?"

"There is more hope in warfare than importing and exporting negroes."

"This continent is a theater for war between nations all over the world."

"How is fighting a war supposed to restore the failing fortunes to the African Company?"

"Jamaica needs negroes to work on sugar plantations."

"Africa needs negroes to develop the gold mines and other labor."

"Both them and us want a war to collect what is rightfully ours."

"War will bring wealth to the community of the winner and destruction for the looser."

"I am ready to make a decision," Obi Mberekpe said.

"I want every village in Iboland to engage in making preparations for war with the Royal Jamaican Company.

Beat the royal war drums so loud that nothing but "preparation for war" can be heard in Iboland. Get my iron gong, "the king's mouth and voice," and announce that I hereby declare war against the Royal Jamaican Company. Organize "warrior associations" in every community that will be available to go to war. Collect a "grand army" of Ibo warriors throughout Iboland to meet me at the banks of the Niger River. Tell the women to prepare the war canoes to meet all vessels that have sailed from the West Indies. Burn down any forts and factories built or owned by any foreigners on our settlement. Give presents, money, and loans to the rulers of any kingdom and their natives who will help us win the war. Get hundreds of soldiers to guard the castle in my absence. Meet me at the ancestral shrine to "beg the ghosts" for victory," then Obi Mberekpe and his administraton collectively signed and delivered a letter at the meeting that stated, "The village of Mbubu is prepared for a war with the Royal Jamaican Company."

The drums beat and the flutes sang "The King Of Slaves."

"Blessed with a "treasure-house of riches," every morning between six and eight o'clock country women and children may be seen riding into the marketplace to sell everything from fruits and vegetables to firewood and charcoal on a land that has wealth, history, and a tradition that attracts people from continents all over the world, especially those looking for sugar-cane plantations, yet the mysterious and fascinating country has an air of revolution and war."

"It was during the sixteenth century when the French

claimed to have brought thousands of black people who were holding on to their mother religion, their chief's black magic, the voodoo of witch doctors of the African jungles and their ancestors from the Congo, and all parts of Africa on hundreds of ships driven by thousands of explorers who landed on an island settled by pirates."

"Negroes were being imported by the shiploads from Africa to an island where every faithful negro who performed all the work in all parts of the island of African slaves and French upper-class fought for their freedom, proclaimed himself the king or the president or the general of the man-made tropical jungle of fertile fields of a civilization that was seized by the French who named it "Domingue, Le Pays de Revenants," "The Country of the Ghosts," or the country you are bound to come back to."

"Which ghost walks the jungles and mountains at night?"

"Le Ferriere, King Christophe, King Henri I, Henri Christophe, Haiti's black master, King of Black Slaves, the former negro slave who enslaved thousands of men who lived in fear of disobeying his royal will and walked the old royal road carrying half a million tons of building material up the side of a mountain through jungles and deep, steep back-breaking slopes to build a castle and return to the bottom of the mountain in Haiti's wilderness to take a cannon back up the top of the mountain and leave it in his palace, "The Citadel," as the king worked his troops mercilessly to build his Egyptian Pyramid."

The drummer sits beneath the tree with a tom-tom. The beat of the drum comes faintly across the quiet waters of Africa to the ends of the earth. He listens to the sounds of his tom-tom that can be heard from Haiti to Africa and from Africa to Haiti. It sounds far away when close at hand and close at hand when far away.

Obi Mberekpe and his warriors met at the banks of the Niger River in war canoes to join together with other kings, chiefs, and as many members of the community in Iboland who would join them. They gathered together at a camp in a secret place in the forest where the Royal Jamaican Company's vessels were supposed to appear after the ancestral shrine ceremony took place. The village of Mbubu's war canoes were equipped with a medicinal shield that was believed to make the soldiers invisible to the enemy. All wars were fought in the name of the king, so the community paraded to the war cult, a place where devotion takes place before a war, with their war drums and horns to pay tribute to him. When the king shoved his "ceremonial sword" to the ground, everybody present knew that he was declaring a war. Before they prayed at the ancestral shrine, the senior priest began the ceremony by breaking a kola nut and offering palm-oil to the war spirits.

"Ikenga, we pray for the success of this ceremony."

"Ikenga, we pray for the war spirits that are about to lead us."

"Ikenga, we pray for the guidance of the ancestors and their protection."

"Ikenga, help the queen prepare the women of the community."

"Ikenga, give the queen power through the charms that go with her title."

"Ikenga, make the African Company victorious in this war against the Royal Jamaican Company."

"Akameigbo," "The king is the one who will win a battle against the enemy."

"Akameigbo," "The king is the great warrior of the community."

"Akameigbo," "The king is worshipped."

"Akameigbo," "We praise your name."

"Akameigbo," "The king is above all mortals."

The "First Great War" on the continent of Africa was fought with great bitterness for three days. The Royal Jamaican Company believed this trip to be their last slave voyage as they joined forces with more than 50 ships to get as many negroes as possible from the African Company. Armies of several thousand men took the battlefield that day, but the war canoes and weapons used by the Africans were not enough to overpower the enemy. Hundreds of negroes were enslaved for money that was not paid to the Royal Jamaican Company as punishment for something, or they became prisoners of war on slave vessels that left Africa after the war. The Royal Jamaican Company was victorious, and the African warriors were driven off to their neighboring towns and villages for protection from danger. There is an African proverb that goes, "If two pots collide, the smaller one must break."

The drums beat and the flutes sang at the end of the war.

"Odibo jele uno," "The sevant has gone home."

The last festival that took place in the village of Mbubu was on the day that the Royal Palace realized that Obi Mberekpe had disappeared. His royal servants went looking for him.

"Where is the king?"

"Has he gone on to become a hidden king of his clan?"

"He was not at the Royal Palace this morning."

"The throne can never be left vacant."

"There will be much conflict in the community if there is no Obi on the throne."

"His disappearence must be kept a secret."

"It will be a terrible event if the king does not appear."

"The king never dies."

Today was the day the messengers of the king's household followed the custom of informing the important members of society to gather together at the Royal Palace for a collective ritual. Go-di-di-go-di-go. Di-go-do-di-go. Everybody in Iboland who understood the language of the hollowed-out wooden instrument showed up at the Royal Palace that morning. Two slaves, one on each side of the palaces chamber door, received the royal guests.

"There is no weeping or feelings of sadness at the king's throne."

"Anyone present today who raises an alarm of either kind will be made to pay a fine of the price of a cow."

"If you need to cry, do so secretly."

The two slaves closed the chamber door of the Royal Palace. The guests followed the slaves through the chamber to a throne that was on top of a platform with the emblems of the king's office, the royal ufie drum, the leopard skin, the sword, the crown, the king's robes, eagle feathers, a fan made from the skin of an animal, and a horn made from elephant's tusks. When all of the people assembled at the palace, palm-oil and kola nuts were offered, prayers were made to the ancestors, and the breaking of kola nuts was distributed according to their age and seniority. My mother and the rest of my family sat down on a mat that was spread on the king's throne. A big basin of water was placed before the throne. We dipped our hands in the water and washed our faces to show that we had wept for my father. The water was thrown out and kola nuts and cowries were put on a plate and placed before the throne in case the king showed up for something to eat. A cannon was fired in the village square to inform the public that I would be representing my father until the next Obi was installed.

The "Itikpo Ukpo," "the breaking down of the throne," ceremony was held on the next morning to lead the Obi's spirit to the other world where it would join the past Obis. Before the war, dancers displayed their swords, shields, and other weapons of war. I had to dance as my father did before becoming an Obi at his installation ceremony. Royal dancing groups dressed in war-like clothes and staged a variety of dances, but the most important dance was the dance of the extraordinary ability of the king's warriors on land and on water. The elders displayed their war canoes. The women prepared a feast of seven cows – one for the title society, one for the elders, one for the ikenga, one for their Chi, one for the family of the king, one for the community, and one for the chiefs. Each group was given seven kola nuts, seven yams, and seven bottles of palm-oil. After the communal feast, the egwugwu, a masquerader, pretended to be one of the ancestral spirits of the village. A special masked egwugwu danced to represent the king, the other masked egwugwus danced to represent the spirits of past kings. The occasion of rejoicing can take place for as long as a month to three years or until a new king is selected and crowned.

The drums beat and the flutes sang "The Native African Radio."

"The Native African Radio transmits messages that can be heard over a land of dark, silent nights where every animal from an alligator to a zebra made its home and fearless hunters with long spears for weapons."

"Villages with huts cleared fields filled with people growing corn, rice, sesame, peanuts, corn, and brown beans."

"From cocks-crow until the chickens went to roost, hundreds of women worked in their stalls selling tropical fruits, cacao, rubber, and goatskins to furnish Nigeria's famous Moroccan leather that is prepared to be carried to the outdoor markets where it will be fleshed, tanned, and dyed red, green, and brown."

"The exploration began on December 1922 and ended on January 1923."

"As far as the eye could see, civilization disappeared for hundreds of miles until there was nothing but sand and rocks."

"Days slipped into weeks, and weeks slipped into months that led to another longer journey made by heavy-laden camels whose hooves sank into the sandy ground carrying men to North Africa."

"The road begins with crossing Mali, Benin, Nigeria, Niger, Chad, Sudan, Egypt, Libya, Tunisia, Algeria,

Morocco, and Mauritania thousands of miles on camel's backs or by motor car."

"Parties of tribesmen and foreigners ride their camel's backs that change into cars that ride into the gates of Morocco in North Africa after making their camps in swamps, forests, and palm trees."

"Donkeys and camels that follow camels carrying tropical fruit, vegetables, peppers, grain, peanuts, cotton, palm-oil, kernels, rubber, spice, yams, dyed cotton cloth, and kola nuts."

"Servants and followers of their merchant owners ride together on camel's backs singing songs of the terrors of their journey crossing East Africa to North Africa."

"Still I rise with the sun," "Glory to Allah for light and darkness."

"The French built military posts to stop raids and made the same journey in automobiles."

"The Europeans captivated the most mysterious continent on the planet in pictures."

"The North Africans – white-skinned Arabs, brown-skinned Berbers, and black-skinned slaves."

"Houses made out of camel-skinned tents near rocks and cactus in sand dunes underneath the heavens full of shooting stars."

"The waters of the Atlantic Ocean smell like salt and shine like emeralds, sapphires, and opals."

"As we get closer to the greatest and wealthiest cities in Africa, we look for signs of first-fruits harvest festivals – a celebration of their greatest treasure, agriculture."

"The country of the "true faith," the kingdom that has held out longer than any other kingdom in Africa."

"The oldest of the imperial cities of the first Arab dynasty of Morocco, an Arabian city where pilgrims once worshipped in the shrines, a history of famous universities and colleges, shop-lined streets that were once mixed with people, donkeys, horses, sheep, dogs, mules, and black slaves."

"The faithful worshipers of Allah, the one who made the heaven above and the earth beneath the sea, and all that is thereof, speaking greetings from the Koran."

"The most important call of every day from the top of a mosque."

"La il-ah-il-ah-Allah
Mohammad ar-ra-sou-la Allah
Allah is Allah! There is no God but Allah
Mohammed is the Prophet of God."

"Alleys filled with shops selling textiles, crafts, jewelry, brass, wood, cloth, copper, carpets, pottery, wool, and sheep skins."

"Servants and the followers of their merchant owners singing songs and telling folktales taught to them by their ancestors."

"Meknes held me within its seven gates that were closed to long lines of camels carrying tribesmen from Nigeria and other parts of Africa waiting patiently for them to open."

"The desert caravan traders meet at the open market to discss the price of Moroccan leather, but nothing is bought without the exciting experience of bargaining from merchants who work from sunrise to sunset looking for the best price for their goods until the day at the stalls comes to an end."

"The hour of sunset prayer approaches, as the last piece of Moroccan leather has been sold and the crowd gives praise to Allah who in his wisdom sends good days and bad days, scatters about before retiring to their homes as the caravan loads up their camel's backs for the long journey through the deserts and jungles of North Africa."

# CHAPTER 7

An old man once said, "When two elephants fight, it is the grass that gets trampled." He was talking about the rumors of war between the Royal Jamaican Company and the African Company. On the morning after the war ended in the village of Mbubu, the sound of an iron gong filled the air. Gome, gome, gome, gome, gome, gome, gome boomed the hollow metal of the town crier's ogene setting up a wave of expectation in the crowd, followed by the voice of the messenger, "The Company of Merchants trading to Africa has landed at the Niger River to ship survivors of the war to the Carribean." As many negroes as possible – men, women, boys, and girls – were packed on board the vessels for the voyage to the colonies for safety. I was separated from my family when the ship left, but I can remember the voices of people who were on the ship.

"I heard we will be dropped off the ship in Jamaica."

"I would rather stay in Iboland."

"The village of Mbubu has been destroyed."

"There are rumors of earthquakes on islands."

"An earthquake can sink a whole city."

"We could end up anywhere from London to Spain at the end of this voyage."

"Between now and the next 100 years, over 500,000 negroes will be shipped to Jamaica from Africa."

"At the Jamaican slave sales, we will know who is the most valuable."

"The tribesmen of the Gold Coast, the Ashanti, and Fanti are already the most valuable negroes."

"The Yoruba tribesmen and Ibo come next in value."

"The Fulani tribesmen and the Mandingoes of Sierra Leone are also represented among Jamaican slaves."

"The slave traders are afraid to explore the Gambia."

"They are considered to be the most dangerous and difficult to capture."

"The Company of Merchants heard rumors that the negroes who live anywhere near there are dangerous."

"The Jamaicans are from Africa brought as slaves to work on plantations."

"In Iboland, the slaves worked for us."

"A long time ago, negro slaves on these vessels were shackled together."

"Some of the negro slaves on these vessels were enemy tribes with one another in Africa."

"We can feed them ackee fruit and saltfish before they reach the Carribean."

"They can be fed, bathed, and prepared for sale once they reach the Carribean."

"I miss having more than two meals of beans and yams a day."

"Some of these negroes will not survive the sugar-cane plantations on the islands."

"This ship is packed with ivory, cloth, cotton, wood, indigo, and hundreds of negroes."

"Storms and overcrowded conditions will ruin or destroy many ships before they get to where they are headed."

"Before we reach the Carribean, poor white people will get on board who have been forced out of England."

"Some of them fled the war between England and Ireland."

"Others are going to the Carribean to look for work."

"Our heritage of telling folktales about the motherland will be lost."

"What is going to happen to what we believe in?"

"What we believe in will be lost on this vessel."

"The spirits of the ancestors are back there."

"You might see a duppy at night in Jamaica."

"What are duppies?"

"The ghosts of Jamaica."

When I told folktales on the slave ship to Jamaica, a group of boys gathered around me and gave me the nickname "Radio" because I loved to talk so much. In the afternoon, we sang songs and listened to folktales like the one about a king who wanted to stop the slave trade in Africa. Once there was a merchant who did not understand why the king wanted to stop slave trade, so he decided to pay him a visit. "I want you to make war upon the sea-side king who is carrying on the slave trade on the islands. It is customary to declare war every twenty years, and this year is the twentieth year," the king said. When the merchant returned to the islands, he fought a war at sea from a vessel with the sea-side king whose army rode ponies bareback beneath the sea. The merchant sent a letter back to the king to tell him about the war that read, "I ordered my army to block the creeks and rivers, sent my slaves from the sugar-cane plantation to raid the bottom of the sea, and ordered hundreds of canoes to attack the sea-side king." The number of people who came to the sea-side never returned. The king was trying to keep trade in his own hands, so before he left Africa, he made an offering of sticks, rags, fruit, and meat to the water spirits for a safe journey. He ordered war canoes to travel with him up the Niger River, the Benue, the Sokoto, the Kadina, the

Antonio, the Anambara, the Cross River, the Kwa-Ibo, the Brohemie Creek, Benin River, and Calabar River looking for the merchant.

Along the banks of the river, streams, creeks, and sea lies the offerings made by the king before he left Africa and the vessel belonging to the merchant. People said that the merchant was captured, became a puppet in the hands of the king, the merchant survived the king's attack and established himself somewhere else, the king's slaves took a bribe from the merchant to rescue him, or the king and the merchant met one another and later settled the matter at a village some miles from the Benin River. Every twenty years, the ghost of the merchant haunts the king's village. It can be seen on "Ghost's Road," a land that turns soft underneath your feet as it sucks a person beneath the earth and walks towards an evergreen forest near the Cross River at night to conduct a ceremonial battle for fishing grounds.

As night fell, the slave vessels had to reach a seaport market before arriving in Jamaica. Once the vessel reached Jamaica, everybody on board was taken to the plantations where men, women, and children, who were on board the ship that carried them across the ocean, were separated from one another. Everybody joined the first slaves on the island, the Arawak and Taino Indians, who called their homeland Xayamaca, the land of wood, water, rivers and springs, and the Carib Indians who worked like negro slaves in Africa from cock-crow until the chickens went to roost. In Jamaica, the white planter gave light duties in his house to the slaves he preferred over black field slaves, or gave them their freedom with a piece of land to work for themselves. The average estate had 250 to 300 slaves and men, women, and children worked together in crowds clearing the bush with their axes and machetes and digging ditches with hoes. The men and women were put to planting and cutting in the sugar-cane fields, and the older women and children did the weeding until harvest time came. Some of the men were taught how to work as masons and carpenters.

Today, I work for the Holiday Inn Sunspree Resort in Montego Bay as a chauffeur. The ride from Kingston to Montego Bay is a narrow and steep road that goes up then twists and turns past crowded workers who call themselves "Afro-Jamaicans." They remind me of Africa and its people. Some of them are tall, like the slender tribesmen from Sierra Leone, and some of the shorter ones remind me of the Ashanti tribesmen because slaves from many tribes in West and Central Africa were introduced to the islands to cultivate agriculture.

The Rose Hall Great House in Montego Bay was built in the eighteenth century. It is one of the finest private residences of all Jamaica's great houses and is considered to be the most famous great house on the island with the same number of windows, doors, and stair-cases as the number of days in a year, a week, and months. Over 2,000 slaves worked for the owner on that plantation. Jamaica's rich history includes fables and folktales. There is a very old story about the legend of Annie Palmer, the wife of the owner of the Rose Hall Great House. People say her slaves haunt the house and surrounding lands after dark, and that is just one of a number of tales about her life. Annie Palmer was raised in Haiti, another island not far from Jamaica. As a child, she learned a religion from the negro slaves called voodoo, a black magic with witch doctors in the jungles of Africa, and she fell in love with its magic. When Annie Palmer moved to Jamaica with her family, she brought the African folk magic with her, but she was very spoiled and wanted everything she asked for. She would even terrorize the negro slaves on the plantation with the voodoo. After she passed away, duppies – unfriendly, restless spirits that followed slave ships to the Carribean from Africa that roam around scaring people, slamming doors upsetting chairs, and drawing bed curtains – paid her a visit at the Rose Hall Great House. The plantation owner was terrorized by the duppies visiting the estate and called on the negro slaves for help.

"I need your help to get rid of the ghost of Annie Palmer so that I can rest," the plantation owner said.

"Annie Palmer taught us Obeah!" one of the negro slaves said.

"What in the world is Obeah?" the plantation owner asked.

"She told us that it is a magic that can perform certain acts."

"It was a source of strength for negro slaves in Africa."

"The Obi used Obeah as a powerful way of making his slaves obey him."

"Some of the slaves called the Obi an Obeah, which means magician."

"How do I get an Obeah?" the plantation owner asked.

"You have to consult with an Obeahman, a priest, who gets his power from praying to the spirits."

"Where is he?" the plantation owner asked.

The plantation owner and the negro slaves walked together into the sugar-cane plantation and began to worship a wild dance so the Obeahman would help him. That night while the plantation owner and the negro slaves were in the fields dancing, Annie Palmer rode up to the door of the Rose Hall Great House on a black horse and walked through the main hall to the back entrance of the plantation.

"The owner of the Rose Hall Great House wishes to keep Annie Palmer away from the estate with your magic," one of the negro slaves said.

"The Obeah is a good magic when it is used to do good

things, but it is evil when it is used to do evil things. Pick the fruit from the ackee tree and make the plantation owner a drink. Tell him to make a wish before he drinks it. He must be very careful about what he is wishing for. Unless he makes his wishes clear, he will be disappointed," the Obeahman said.

"How do we know when the drink is casting a spell on him?"

"The ackee drink will make him unable to speak for up to eight hours. It is called a "curse of dumbness," the Obeahman said.

The slaves were afraid of the magic of the Obeah, so they did as they were told. Annie Palmer watched as the negro slaves prepared the drink from the ackee fruit and served it to the plantation owner. He fell asleep and never woke up. So if you are in Montego Bay at night, beware of the duppies.

There is another story about her life in Jamaica. Annie Palmer was raised in Haiti in a well-to-do valley home with servants who lived in the hills with over three million people who lived from the earth plowing, sowing, and raising crops. Unlike the settlers who have never done any work with their hands, the Haitian servants who came from West Africa worked on her families farm six days a week cultivating strawberries, pears, peaches, sugar, coffee, cotton, cocoa, indigo, and tobacco. Annie's parents, like many other settlers, were in Haiti to import and export the products the servants raised for them and sell the crops in the marketplace.

On the seventh day of the week, the servants rested from working and attended a worship ceremony at their church, but the night before the ceremony, the people practiced Obeah. Every day, they sat together at an ingathering of the community at sundown after work. The women prepared the feast, and the men sat around and shared stories with one another, while the children played games. At the end of the feast, the farm folks danced to the beat of their drums and told stories.

One day, the Obeahman told one of the Haitian servants to give Annie Palmer a Wanga doll for her sixteenth birthday. A Wanga doll could bring you love, money, good fortune, bad luck, what you wished for, and other magical charms. The servant gave Annie Palmer a Wanga doll to bring her love, and she became possessed by a love spell. When she moved to Jamaica with her family, she made a wish to fall in love, but she failed to make her wish clearly understood. Annie Palmer got her wish, and she fell in love many, many times. Some of them were slaves who worked on the Rose Hall Great House plantation, and she got married four times.

"You said your name means "out of war peace comes." My name is Lyndon Johnson. I was named after President Lyndon Baine Johnson of the United States of America."

"In Iboland, a child's name is given to the child because of what the name means to the history of the family. Children are given names for almost everything imaginable, especially when it takes place at the time the baby is born."

"We are almost at the Holiday Inn Sunspree Resort."

"You are a good driver."

"The most important thing to remember when driving in Jamaica is that here, we drive on the left side of the road."

"You speak good English."

"The official language of Jamaica is English, but most Jamaicans converse with one another speaking Patois."

"I have told you who I am, now tell me more about you, sir. Why are you in Jamaica?"

"To invest in real estate."

"The government welcomes investors with open arms."

"I heard that the island is one of the biggest business centers in the Carribean."

"Jamaica is an excellent place for doing business."

"We don't get weather like this in the states."

"Everything for the visitor begins here."

"Montego Bay is the main attraction of the future plans of businessmen."

"How do you like Jamacia, Aghagbolu?"

"Jamaica, "Mo Bay" some people call it, is indeed a tropical delight for sun-worshippers."

"The different races of people who live here today is amazing to me."

"Our motto is "Out of Many, One People," a combination of African, English, Spanish, Arabic, Chinese, Indian, Irish, Scottish, German, Lebanese, Syrian, and others."

"It is a cultural medley."

"This island is my home. My favorite food is "the king of crops," the yam, and it is cultivated here. I can remember going to the marketplace in the village of Mbubu with my mother for sugar, yams, cassava, fruits, vegetables, spices, cocoa, and pimentos. The yam season here is from January to July, about the same time of the year as in my village. In Jamaica, sugar is king."

"You have said that you are from Iboland?"

"Yes sir. I was born over there."

"Did you know that Christopher Columbus visited this island after 1492, and called it "El Golfo de Bueon Tiempo," "good weather gulf?"

"Yes, it is hot year round here."

"I see why Christoper Columbus loved this land."

"In one of his letters during his exploration of the bay, he wrote, "Jamaica is the fairest isle that eyes have beheld.""

"I plan to rebuild the old parts of the island."

"We could use more hotels, shops, and restaurants."

"Life doesn't look easy here for the negro."

"That is true sir, but there is a song about our struggles that we sing."

"Hang on, come a rain come shine
Whenever there is a storm
I know they've got to be a calm
Hang on, come a rain come shine
We'll soon see dawn
Cause although its windy not warm
Ji will guide us through the storm."

"Although life is hard here, like Anancy, the famous folk hero spider, the negro will survive."

"It is true that a people that loves freedom will in the end be free."

"A country can be destroyed, but the Jamaican spirit is indestructible."

Jamaica has been an excellent place to do business since the times of pirates, the early adventurers of the Carribean, like Blackbeard, the king of the Carribean Waters, Morgan, and Kidd, who legend tells us pirated the Carribean in search of gold until the revolt of Mother Earth, a tremendous earthquake that shook Port Royal leaving nothing but a trace of civilization above water. Centuries ago, Jamaica was a pirates Babylon in the last days of piracy before the earthquake shook the island and sent pirates into the sea. "Fallen Jerusalem" and other ghost ships waited until a full moon, and the spirits of ghosts returned to recover the silver, gold, and pearls they lost. They hid like sea-wolves along Seven Mile Beach in Negril from the ghost of Blackbeard, who carried a purse full of gold bracelets, his neck was decorated with gold chains, and he was there to spy out vessels. When it was safe to carry whatever treasure they found to another island, usually Haiti, they divided it among other spirits. That is the reason why people called them the "real governors" of the magical island of sapphire and emerald coasts and water that is clear enough for light to pass through. There are hundreds of rivers here in Jamaica. Black River Jamaica is one of them. Before slavery was abolished, put to an end, the Black River was an important port for slave trade. One of the most feared rivers in Africa is called "JuJu Rock." On a small island in Nigeria that was good for slave trading, hundreds of womenfolk paddled their way through grasslands and swamps from up the creeks and rivers to gather together like a church congregation bringing vegetables, fruit, fish, poultry, eggs, grain, cereal, homespun native-dyed and imported cloth, and firewood from the deep forests to sell at the markets. There was another market, a medicine mart, that was amazing to the native tribes. You could purchase herbs, oils, feathers, bones, teeth, fur, feet, and claws of birds and beasts to cure sick people. Most of the travelers were women who traveled some distance from their village communities to get to the markets. They had no fear because their juju is supposed to protect them. On the other hand, lurking in the Atlantic Ocean sailing towards the African harbor was a ship packed with European merchants from the other side of the world who explored the island like the Israelites in Exodus who saw manna from heaven, the Nigerian woman, her commodities, and agricultural products. The business of life was mixed with trade where either the European merchants who were fascinated by the way natives live, or the women traders who would dare turn down an opportunity to make their fortunes in a land that is filled with milk and honey. There is an African proverb that goes, "Beware and take heed of the Bight of Benin, where few come out, though many go in."

"You have taught me one of the best history lessons I have learned in my entire life in a few hours. What else can I do in Montego Bay when I am not sunning on the beaches besides visit the Rose Hall Great House?"

"Some of the most fabulous golf courses in the Carribean are on this island, or you can take a ride up the Black River on a safari, famous for American crocodiles. Do you know anything about a safari in Africa?"

"I know that a safari is a hunting trip."

"I know a story about a river safari. Would you like to hear it?"

"Why not?"

One day, a baby gorilla, an elephant, a crocodile, a hippopotamus, an antelope, a rhinocerous, a chimpanzee, and a cow decided to cross the Benue River in Africa for the first time. The eight animals fashioned a raft out of five or six large dugout canoes lashed together with a platform built over the whole raft. If the canoes were large enough, or if they could get enough of them, the raft would be strong enough to support several loaded trucks. Natives crossing the Benue River lost a half a day getting the whole safari over the wide river.

"If the river is not deep, we can cross it with a pole," the baby gorilla said.

"If the river is deep enough we can cross it with a paddle," the elephant said.

"This looks like a clumsy vessel," the crocodile said.

"We have created a canoe to operate like a human machine," the hippopotamus said.

"It will be impossible to do this job without music," the antelope said.

"That is easy in this land," the rhinocerous said.

"I love jazz music," the chimpanzee said.

"Let's create a rhyme to help us move the canoe," the cow said.

"We will need two drums and an orchestra," the baby gorilla said.

"You be the soprano," the elephant said to the crocodile.

"You be the alto," the hippopotamus said to the antelope.

"You be the tenor," the rhinocerous said to the chimpanzee.

"I will be the baritone," the cow said.

The eight animals climbed on board the raft. The elephant was the paddler, the hippopotamus and the chimpanzee were the drummers for the job of getting across the wide river, and the rest of the animals were the orchestra. As the raft moved across the muddy stream from hundreds of miles away, the animals could hear the booming of drums and the praise songs of an African tribe that mixed with the voices of their orchestra. The river they were crossing was a lot like the Black River in Jamaica. It was known for having hundreds of crocodiles, some of them as long as 18 to 25 feet long that sun themselves on a midstream sand bank and hippopotamuses who went into the river because they were curious about the canoes that drifted across it. The orchestra of animals, the drummers, and the paddler accomplished their melodious task of working together harmoniously at the same speed during their safari until one of them spotted a hunter in a raft on a safari looking for a gorilla and an elephant. The crocodiles in the river continued to sun themselves on the midstream sun bank, but a hippopotamus who had been playing in the river was underneath the raft that the hunter was in. When the hippopotamus came up above the water, he bumped into his raft causing it to turn over. The hunter fell into the river. The baby gorilla, the elephant, the crocodile, the hippopotamus, the antelope, the rhinocerous, the chimpanzee, and the cow lost half a day getting the whole safari over the wide river, but they lived happily ever after.

One day, a baby gorilla, a chimpanzee, a full-grown African bull elephant, and a cow wandered into the camp of their owner, a West African king. While the baby gorilla sat at the table eating some leftovers from a plate with a spoon, the chimpanzee drank milk from a bottle, the full-grown African bull elephant drank spirits and watched for the West African king to return, and the cow untied a knot that untangled the rope that held the tent together causing it to collapse on top of everybody. After hours of recovering from their unexpected surprise, the West African king discovered what they had done. He decided to send them on a journey with cameras and ordered the animals not to return home until they proved their respect and nobility towards him by taking pictures of another West African king who lived hundreds of miles away from his kingdom. An army of fifteen thousand men with leopard skins over their shoulders greeted the animals at the gates of the West African king's Royal Palace. The palace slaves ushered the baby gorilla, the chimpanzee, the full-grown African bull elephant, and the cow into a large hut that rested in the center of the compound where they waited for His Majesty.

"Your army has reached us many moons journey away," one of the king's slaves said.

"Your Highness has arranged for you to view the palace in the morning," another one of the king's slaves said, then they disappeared into the night as they crossed the courtyard.

The next morning, the baby gorilla, the chimpanzee, the full-grown African bull elephant, and the cow were awakened by drums, tom-toms, brass instruments, and flutes in the compound. The army returned, but this time they surrounded the West African king who was being escorted in a private vehicle. There was a parade of dancers and entertainers with spears and shields made out of rhinocerous hides saluting the king. The baby gorilla, the chimpanzee, the full-grown African bull elephant, and the cow raced for their cameras, but could only get pictures of what looked like a sea of black faces, flashing swords, waving spears, and shields. It was not until noon that the animals were able to focus their cameras on the king. The West African king got out of the vehicle and posed for the animals. The baby gorilla's picture was of the king standing before him in a purple and red robe. The chimpanzee's picture was of the king's huge ostrich-feather sandals on his feet. The full-grown African bull elephant's picture was of the king and his nobles. The cow's picture was of the king standing with a royal bodyguard on each side of him. It was evening before the parade passed the animal's hut, and they were able to get a good night's rest. At cocks-crow, the baby gorilla, the chimpanzee, the full-grown African bull elephant, and the cow gathered together their cameras and left the compound to go back home to their master. The West African king was amazed when he saw the pictures that the animals showed him. The king granted the animals their freedom, and the baby gorilla, the chimpanzee, the full-grown African bull elephant, and the cow fled to the jungle where they lived happily ever after.

There is another folktale about three native boys who took a camel caravan across the "sand ocean" south of Algeria, the country of their desert garden and rolling sand dunes – sand piled up by the wind to the nearest oasis – to get to a well that kept trees and vegetation alive. Their camels reached a large sand dune, a "moving capital" of a collection of low camel-skin tents where they met a camel butcher who had two trucks and a car.

"I will give you one truck for your camels," the camel butcher said to the three native boys.

The three boys filled up their bags with water and drove away faithfully in the truck. The road back home was difficult, even riding in trucks or cars. It rains only once every two or three years in the middle of the Sahara, so when it does rain, nature makes up for lost time. In a few moments, as far as the eye could reach, there was nothing but sand and rocks that changed into a rushing stream of water. Mud and stones trapped them in the truck, but the rushing stream of water was far greater, and it managed to carry them back to the top of the Sahara. There is an Algerian proverb that goes, "Allah has said, "Start moving so that I may start blessing."

"Would you like to hear a folktale about the magic of Iboland?"

"Of course I would, Aghagbolou."

A handful of about 300 "great white lords" lived luxuriously among a huge town of some 80,000 natives where they played cricket, polo, and tennis at a country club. The natives were ruled by a chief who lived a short distance away. About two hours distance from the chief lived a king who had nearly two million subjects. An ambassador of the chief sent an army to deliver a message to the king's imperial court that the "great white lords" were coming to visit him and they would not arrive empty-handed. The "jungle wireless" signal of the village drums carried the message from the chief across the river to the king who returned the message with a signal from his palace drums that the "great white lords" were welcome at his kingdom. The king called on a witch doctor whose religion was magic and said, "Show me everything you see the "great white lords" doing."

The road to the king's palace was excellent enough to drive a car, so the "great white lords" took gifts to present to the king. They carried a camera to take pictures and a tape recorder to make a record of everything they heard. The party saw 200 horsemen of the king's royal guards standing in front of a resthouse wearing rainbow colored costumes and carrying spears, a collection of mud carved huts that covered as much ground as Buckingham Palace, the king's palace, the throne room with mud walls, a ceiling painted with different colors of silver, the king, his nobles, his court, his slaves, his army, his city, and his people came forward to greet the "great white lords." The guests presented gifts of a suit of armour with a helmet and sword, jewelry, flashlights, matches, and a small cannon to the king. The king's slaves presented gifts of peanuts, rice, potatoes, woven grass mats, spears, bows, arrows, leopard skins, and more food than the "great white lords" could carry home.

"I possess unlimited power over my subjects, but the "great white lords" possess a "white magic" that is unknown to me," the witch doctor explained to the king.

"What is the name of the "white magic?"

"It is a magic box."

Upon hearing the witch doctor, the "great white lords" took out their cameras and started taking pictures of the king and his city. They took out a tape recorder and told the king to say a few words into the microphone, then they played their recording back to him. He was so enchanted and overcome by their magic when they gave him a picture and a recording of the tape, he placed them in a sacred pouch that was filled with his other most prized treasures. An army of thousands of soldiers escorted the "great white lords" back home to the river frontier. There is an African proverb that goes, "To have no enemies is equivalent to wealth."

"What are those sayings you call proverbs at the end of your stories?"

"Proverbs are the "breath of speech in Africa." The speaker uses proverbs to teach a lesson about good behavior."

"Do you ever think about leaving Jamaica?"

"I dream about moving to America, but I long to return to the motherland, the land of my ancestors."

"What do you miss about Africa the most?"

"The Yam Festival that is held at harvest time. Hundreds of family members gather together with yams in baskets and palm-oil, and they leave home to go to the center of the compound. It is customary to pour libations every day before the celebration begins. There are seven libations. A libation is poured on the first day to honor the sons and daughters of Africa from the past, present, and future who worked from sunrise to sunset in the fields to make the harvest of the motherland bountiful. A libation is poured on the second day to give thanks for the harvest and to ask for another year of prosperity. A libation is poured on the third day for paving the road upon which they walk on today. A libation is poured on the fourth day for life. A libation is poured on the fifth day for inspiring the community to be an inspiration to the other people who live in the community. A libation is poured on the sixth day for preserving our heritage and our culture, and a libation is poured on the seventh day for setting an example for the children who will grow up and practice the principles of The Yam Festival in the future."

"Is that the hotel over there?"

"This is the Holiday Inn Sunspree Resort. I will carry your bags to the front desk for you, sir."

"Aghagbolu, it was a pleasure to ride with you from Kingston to Montego Bay. What more can I say?"

"Sad to know that you're leaving sir, but Ji will guide you out and coming in."

"Thank you, Aghagbolu."

Aghagbolu returned back to his limousine, turned on the radio, and listened to the song, "The Border."

"If I could reach the border
Then I would step across
So please take me to the border
No matter whats the cost."